ROBYN LEE

Robyn Lee works for Ben Martin at the Old Admiral Inn, a neglected centre for smuggling on the coast. Her ambition is to bring the inn back to its old popularity, so she agrees when he asks her to run errands. Now she is a smuggler, but when she falls for handsome Daniel Winters, a customs officer, she must make a difficult choice. The surprise revelation of a secret about her birth may just give her the help she needs . . .

CHRISTINA GREEN

ROBYN LEE

Complete and Unabridged

LINFORD
Leicester

First published in Great Britain in 2013

First Linford Edition
published 2015

A catalogue record for this book is available
from the British Library.

ISBN 978–1–4448–2334–9

Published by
F. A. Thorpe (Publishing)
Anstey, Leicestershire

Set by Words & Graphics Ltd.
Anstey, Leicestershire
Printed and bound in Great Britain by
T. J. International Ltd., Padstow, Cornwall

This book is printed on acid-free paper

1

I heard about the position at the old inn as I went into the village to deliver Mrs Hook's clean washing. Two of the old fishermen were gossiping, sitting on the quay mending their nets, and Joe Hannaford said, just as I was passing, 'So now old Cap'n Martin's gone at the inn, his two boys'll take over, and they want a new maid in the taproom, so I heard.'

And Eddy Stringer puffed at his pipe and laughed. 'She'll need a good strong body — all those barrels of ale to be rolled in, and keeping the boys' hands off her as well . . . '

I stopped, put down the laundry basket, and said, 'Reckon I could do the job, do you then, Joe?'

I watched their old eyes gleam as they roared with laughter, before nodding.

'Why not Robyn?' asked Joe. 'You're

a big maid — and I wouldn't want to get on the wrong side of you — 'specially with that head of red hair.'

Yes, I was known for my red head. Ma said that was why they called me Robyn. And Joe was right, I didn't put up with nonsense if I could help it. I thought I'd enjoy working at the inn — lots of talk and they danced sometimes, I'd heard. Of course, there would probably be fights and brawls at times, but the old captain's sons, Ben and Matthew Martin, would deal with that.

A new position! Anything would be better than forever helping Ma with the washing she took in every week. Rinsing, mangling, hanging it out on the line, fetching it in, then heating up irons and smoothing out every single wrinkle — and then the walks to all the houses waiting for clean linen. I'd been Ma's helpmate for almost all of my seventeen and a half years and oh goodness yes, I wanted a change now. Ma would still go on washing, of course, but we had a new neighbour, chatty Molly Black, who seemed keen to help out. So, as I neared Mrs Hook's house, I made up my mind. Once the last delivery of washing was done I would go to the inn and offer my services.

It was mid-afternoon before I left the village and started on the long uphill road to the old inn. I put on a last bit of speed as I turned down the lane sloping to the river and saw the inn ahead of me. There was a man busy on the foreshore in front of the building. I saw him doing repairs to a small dinghy pulled up on the sand — one of the brothers, I thought, who were both local fishermen. I walked towards him, trying to think what I would say. Mustn't be too smart — men didn't like maids who talked too much; I knew that. So when I reached the side of the boat I coughed slightly, and he looked round at me. And frowned.

'What do you want?' This was the elder boy, Ben. He was stocky, with a bit of a stoop because he had a game leg, and a face that clearly wanted to live in his own little world and not be bothered with red-headed girls who were interrupting what he was doing.

I felt the usual quick temper stir inside me. How dare he be so rude when I was here to offer to help him out. But I managed a polite smile and said quietly, 'I hear as you're looking for a new maid in the inn. Well, I can do it. What do you pay?'

'Pay? I wouldn't pay you a penny piece, not a maid with a sharp manner and a red poll.' He straightened up and stared at me with narrowed dark eyes and then, just as I was about to tell him I wouldn't take his horrid old position for any money he liked to offer, he smiled and chuckled and his face took on a new, more friendly look. 'Why, it's Robyn Lee, I do believe. And we all know what you and your red head's like — a bit bossy. Well, you might even make a good inn maid. Don't take no nonsense, do you?'

'No,' I said, holding my breath very tightly and getting ready to walk away if he said another nasty word. Bossy, was I? 'I'm a good worker,' I said sharply. 'But I won't be spoken to rude-like. If I work for you, Ben Martin, you'll have to keep a civil tongue in your head.' And I met his staring eyes, dared him to smile any more, and waited with my hands clenched into tight fists.

He went on staring, but his expression softened. 'My old dad,' he said at last, 'liked a maid who answered back. Maybe I'll take you on, just to please him, even though he's gone. See, my brother Matt and me plan to make this inn a busy old place to bring in more folk. Make more money. Well, p'raps we need a hothead like you to help things along. All right then, so when can you start, Robyn Lee?'

Inside me the hot temper faded into small rushes of joy and I smiled sweetly at him. 'If the money's right I could start tomorrow, Ben. How much will it be?'

'Your bedding and your keep, and some warm pennies every Saturday night, if you work well.'

I decided that Ben Martin, after all, was a nice man. I gave him my best smile and nodded, saying airily, 'That'll do me for a start. See how we get along, shall we, then?'

He burst out laughing. 'You'll do,' he said. 'I'll give you a week or two and then maybe we'll think about more pennies. So make sure you're here sharp and early tomorrow morning. There's floors to clean and barrels to bring in and glasses to wash. And food to cook — can you cook?'

'I can do anything,' I said proudly. 'My ma, Mrs Lee, brought me up to be a really useful maid. Yes, I'll be here early. So goodbye for now, Ben Martin.' I turned away and walked back the way I'd come.

I felt like singing, even though the late afternoon was turning grey with a sea fog rolling in. I had a new position! I might even become responsible for running the old inn and make a name for myself. But I had to go home now and tell Ma I was moving out. My huge smile died as I tramped down the long hill, knowing I had two more miles to go. And then, of course, she wouldn't want me to leave.

'Going where?' Ma's husky voice was unnaturally loud and not at all happy.

I smiled at her with all the determination I could get together. 'The Admiral Inn. You know, where Cap'n Martin has just died.'

'Course I know. The whole village knows. Poor old man; he lasted a long time, but now them boys of his do own the inn, what will they do with it? Rough they are, and not above bad things. And you say you're going there? No, Robyn love, you're not leaving us.'

I sucked in a big breath, went over to Ma and put my arms around her. 'Ma, you got to let me go. I'm grown now — eighteen in the autumn — and I need to do something with my life except that awful old washing.'

'No, your life is here, maid. Where it's always been.' Ma had tears in her eyes and I felt my will to leave grow even more determined. Of course I must go. I'd told that Martin chap I'd be there in the morning. So another breath and then, my voice a bit louder, 'Ma, I'm going and that's all there is to say. You want me to have a good life, don't you? And I will — I'll get to clean the old Admiral and make it a proper place ready for people to visit. Why . . . ' Laughing, I tried to force Ma to look into my eyes. 'You love me, like I love you and Father, so just let me go. Please . . . '

Ma sat down heavily and looked towards the door as Father came in from the garden, kicking off his boots and carrying a cabbage and some carrots. 'Maid wants to go and work at the Admiral,' she said tearfully. 'But I can't let her go, can I?'

There was a long pause and I knew there were important thoughts being exchanged, but had no idea why my parents were being so slow and undecided. Until Father put the vegetables in the sink, sat down opposite Ma, and looked across at me. 'You really want to go, maid? You sure you can do all that hard work?'

'Yes, I'm sure. And I'll come home and give you what I earn.'

'We don't want no money, maid. Just need to know that you're safe and . . .' He paused for a long moment, looking at Ma and nodding his head. 'And happy. Important that you're happy, see, like you've always been here with us.'

Why was he wondering about my happiness? Couldn't he see how happy this new job was making me feel? But I was grown, a young woman with a mind of her own, and the new job was offering me an interesting new life. I thought hard for a few minutes, watching Father and Ma as they looked at each other. Ma wiped her eyes and then slowly nodded, while Father put out his hand to reach across the space and touch hers, taut in her lap, and I knew then that something was happening, but had no idea what it could be.

But gradually I saw them both slowly smile and knew excitedly then that my longing for the new job was to be approved, after all.

'Be careful, maid.' Father looked at me with keen eyes and Ma said, 'Those Martin boys aren't all perlite, you know — don't let them be unkind to you. P'raps there'll be someone else working there who'll keep an eye on you.'

I twirled around the small kitchen, excited and sure of myself. 'I don't need anyone else. I shall do it all, so I'd better go and put my things together. Got to be off proper early tomorrow. It's a long walk, see.' I gave them both a final big smile, then stumped up the wooden stairs to put my few belongings into a shawl which I would tie in a bundle and carry over my shoulder.

Tomorrow! Let it be a fine day, with sunshine and a dry path to follow. Let the Admiral be all ready to welcome me

— oh, I couldn't wait to go! But then I had a last thought — why had Ma and Father been so uneasy about my leaving? But then, they were old and had funny thoughts. They would soon get used to me not being here any longer.

I was up with the first pearly light of dawn, getting the fire going and boiling a kettle of water for a cup of tea. I had a thick slice of bread with some lard spread on it, then called goodbye to Ma, still upstairs, and Father, getting ready to go to work, and then had to wait for Ma to come down too. She had her old wrapper around her and her hair was plaited in a long tail, but she was still Ma, her arms warm and her kiss so loving. She hugged me to her, whispering, 'Make sure you're safe and well. And come back to see us soon. And remember, I've got something belonging to you as you gets older — not now, but maybe on your next birthday.'

I said, 'What is it? Why can't I have it

now?' But she smiled, even though there were tears in her eyes, and said, very low, 'Never mind, my little love. It'll be waiting for you back here at home when you're eighteen.'

So I just shrugged my shoulders, gave her another big hug and a kiss, and said, 'Well, I'm off now, Ma. Wish me luck, won't you?'

I stepped out of the door into the misty morning, shawl on my back. At the top of the hill I looked back to where poor old Ma stood, watching me go.

2

By the time I reached the lane slipping down to the mighty river and saw the Admiral — big, shining and gleaming in the rays of sunshine spreading across the water — I was excited and ready for anything. I knocked at the old oak door, but there was no answer. I knocked again. Where was everybody? More knocking, and then I found a small stone and threw it at the window above the door. Still no movement anywhere. I shouted, 'Ben! Matthew! Where are you? Let me in.' But all that happened was a group of seagulls flew down from the chimney, shrieking at me as if demanding their breakfast.

Then I heard a small, high voice from somewhere around the far side of the inn. Someone singing about 'a sprig of thyme'. It was a song I'd heard Ma sing, so I joined in as I went to find the songster. And there, by the pump in the middle of the yard, stood a small girl filling buckets of water and singing her heart out. I stopped and listened. It was like a lark's song, high and simple but so beautiful that I just stood there, waiting for the last bucket to be filled.

The song stopped. The girl must have heard me, for she stopped pumping and turned. At once her little face tightened and she said in a small, high voice, 'Oh, if you please, I'm just taking in the water to get on with washing the pots.' I understood that this girl was used to being badly treated; to being taken for granted and given all the rough work.

I went up to her, smiled, secured my shawl round my shoulders and picked up a full bucket. I said, 'Don't worry, I'll help you. I'm Robyn, the new girl come to work in the tap room. So who are you?'

Her wide hazel eyes were scared, but she said in a tiny voice, fumbling over the long, hard word, 'I'm an ap — p — prentice from the workhouse. I'm

14

Annie, the pot girl. I got to wash all the pots they used last night, and must do it afore Master comes home or he'll give me what-for.'

We walked together towards the open kitchen door, carrying the buckets, and I said very firmly, 'He certainly won't, cos I won't let him. And we'll do the pots together. But first of all we'll have a drink of tea — I've had a long walk to get here and I'm thirsty. So let's put a kettle on the fire, shall we?'

She still looked afraid, so I pushed ahead of her and put my bucket in the stone sink at the side of the kitchen. 'Where's the kettle?' I asked. No answer. But, having lowered her buckets, she fetched a blackened old kettle and I carefully filled it with water. 'Put that on the fire, and then tell me where the tea caddy is.'

'No! No! Not allowed to have tea — Master keeps the key.'

'So Master is very much the master here, is he?' I didn't know what Ben Martin was like, but I didn't think much of him from what I was hearing. I walked to the big hearth and looked up at the shelf running above it. Yes, there was a box with a lock. Must be the tea caddy. Reaching up, I took it down, but she was at my side, almost shivering with fright.

'No, you mustn't — Master won't let anyone touch it besides him.'

'He's not here; he won't know. Get a couple of mugs, Annie, and some milk from the dairy.' While she was away, I pulled a stout pin from my coiled-up hair and opened the caddy. It was easy when you knew how. The first break-in I'd done as a child was when Father hid the few sweets we ever had in a box with a lock.

The tea smelled good, strong and with a deep colour. Slowly the kettle started to boil and I found a big brown teapot on the dresser. By the time Annie came back with mugs and a small jug of milk, I'd made a brew and was sitting by the fire, ready to start sipping and recovering my strength after that long walk.

Annie stared at me. 'But the pots?'

'After we've had our tea. Drink yours up.' I saw her scared expression and added, 'And enjoy it, Annie. Master Ben won't know we've had some of his precious tea — and anyway, very soon, when he's used to me being here, I shall take over all the keys myself.'

She still stared, and her fingers trembled round the steaming mug, so I said gently and with the warmth which I knew she needed, poor little thing, 'Cheer up. Things are going to get better. Much better. You'll see!' I nodded, and slowly I watched her fright lessen until she actually gave me a little smile across the lip of the mug.

There was a knock at the big front door. I put down my mug and went down the shadowy passage to open it. A man waited there. He was tall and rather old, with very grey hair beneath his smart hat, and a costly riding coat over breeches and polished boots. I saw a horse tethered to a post in the yard behind him. Holding his crop in one gloved hand, he looked down at me, frowning a bit, and said in an educated voice, 'Good day. Is Ben Martin here? Or Matthew? I have an appointment to see them.'

He was clearly gentry, so I said politely, 'I'm sorry, sir, but they're not here. I expect them back soon. Please to come in — perhaps I can take a message?'

He looked around the passage, with its shadows and cobwebs hanging from the beams, and I thought that this place wasn't at all where he wished to be. But he nodded and said, 'Very well. I hope they won't keep me waiting long.'

I led him into the taproom, where the fire was burning nicely after a good poke at it to make the kettle boil. I pushed the big captain's chair closer to it. 'Won't you sit here, sir? And can I get you a tankard of ale?' As I spoke, I looked at the gantries and shelves behind the bar counter and saw bottles of spirits hidden away behind the barrels. 'Or brandy, sir? There's a bottle here . . . '

He folded himself into the chair, having brushed off the dust so that it didn't stain the skirt of his coat, and looked around at me. I saw amusement touch his face, but he said sharply, 'Not this early,' and continued looking around the big room. His eyes, almost black and very keen, fell on Annie standing nervously in the far corner by the stone sink, washing pots, and then returned to me.

'Get on with your work,' he said coldly. 'I see there's plenty to be done.'

I turned back from the counter, where I was sorting out the rubbish that lay jumbled along it, and felt my temper rise at the tone in his voice. Without thinking, I said quickly, 'I'm new here, this mess isn't of my making. Before I've been here much longer things will be different. The Admiral is going to have a real clean-up and be ready for new people to come to.' My annoyance made me forget he was gentry, and I added very fast, 'Perhaps you'll like it better then.' I heard Annie give a little squeak of alarm, which made me realise how rude I had been. 'I beg your pardon, sir,' I started, but he gave a loud laugh and turned in his chair to look at me all the better.

'And no doubt I will, my girl. I like the picture you draw of a newly cleaned and more attractive inn. Where did the Martin brothers find you, I wonder? You sound like a streak of sunlight in a grey world. What's your name?'

'Robyn Lee, sir. Down in the village I heard as there was a situation going when the old captain died, and I came and told Ben I wanted to work here. This is my first morning.'

'Told him you wanted to work here, did you? And I suppose he said yes?' There was real amusement now in the deep gravelly voice, and I thought I saw a more friendly gleam in the almost black eyes.

I lifted my head an extra half inch. 'He did — after a bit. Cos I told him I would make the Admiral a place worth visiting.'

'And what did his brother Matthew say, I wonder?'

'I didn't see him. I don't know what he'll think, finding me here.'

There was a pause, so I got on with scouring the stained oak counter with a bowl of water from one of Annie's buckets, and concentrated on my work.

'I imagine he'll be quite surprised.'

I thought I heard a depth of wryness in the words, but kept my head high and told myself that whatever Master Matthew thought or said, I would able to deal with him.

The big door opened with a groan, and footsteps sounded along the passage. Ben appeared and stopped short when he saw the visitor sitting by the fire. 'Mr Winthrop! I hope as I haven't kept you waiting too long? I know it's later than we arranged . . . '

The man — Mr Winthrop — got to his feet and stared down at Ben, who was a good half-head shorter than him.

'Yes,' he said shortly. 'You're certainly late, but I was entertained by this young maid here who, so she says, has it in mind to change the Admiral into a regular visitors' parlour. What do you and your brother think of that, then?'

I sneaked a glance at Ben, who coloured slightly. But he said firmly, 'Robyn has a good idea, sir, and we'll see that she carries it out. It's time the old inn had a new look, for our father, old as he was, and suffering with his breathing, wouldn't make any changes. But now . . . '

'But now.' There was note of something important in the deep voice, and again, as I looked across the room, I saw Mr Winthrop smile and nod his head. Then he looked up, caught my eye, frowned and said rapidly, 'Let us have a quiet word somewhere, Ben. There are plans to make.'

At once Ben moved, gesturing towards the closed door at the side of the taproom, and conducting his visitor there. The door shut after them and

Annie and I looked at each other.

'Secrets,' I said, with a bit of a laugh, disappointed that I wouldn't be able to know what was going on. 'Sounds important, doesn't it? But they won't tell us, of course. We just have to get on with the cleaning.'

Annie gave me her small smile and returned to the pot washing, so I swabbed down the empty counter, giving it all the energy inside me which longed to be in the other room, hearing about the plans they were making.

They seemed to talk for a long time. I had left the taproom and discovered the kitchen before they left the side room. I was firing up the hearth and wondering what I could make out of the almost empty sacks of flour and thin sides of fat bacon hanging from the beams, when I heard their voices as they walked through the taproom, along the passage, and then stood at the door, still talking.

Annie, scraping some rough old turnips and potatoes we found on the larder floor, looked up at me. 'Master Ben'll come in here in a minute — he'll tell us off for drinking his tea.'

I grinned at her. 'Of course he won't. If he does, I'll tell him to cook the dinner himself!' But I found my heart was beating faster as he appeared in the doorway.

He paused just inside the door and stared at Annie, and then at me. 'Mr Winthrop thinks you'll be useful here, Robyn. But we've been talking, and we have to warn you to watch out for certain men who might make a disturbance when they come. Understand me?'

I moved the pan frying onions away from the flame and nodded. 'All right. But you'll be here, won't you, Master? You and your brother. And who are these rough men?'

His face screwed up a bit and he didn't answer. Instead, Mr Winthrop looked at him, and as they left the kitchen, Ben muttered something about, 'One of them's called Daniel

Winters. Not sure about the others.'

When the door shut behind them, I looked at Annie. 'Something's going on, isn't it? Daniel Winters? A rough man, but what a nice name. Well, we can only wait and see.'

3

Night-time: the taproom was emptying of all those noisy, hard-drinking men, and Annie and I were ready for our beds. Matthew had disappeared and Ben Martin was busying himself by the gantry, dealing with empty barrels and dirty pots. I went up to him.

'Can't do no more, Master. We're tired out. We'll do them pots in the morning after we've had a good sleep.'

I turned away, but he stopped me with a snort of laughter and rough words. 'No good being tired, maid. You're here to work, you and that li'l girl. So be down good an' early; I got things to do tomorrow an' I want breakfast afore I go.' Then suddenly, as I walked towards the door, he called me back. 'Which room are you sleeping in?'

I said sharply, 'The one that had the driest bed. Just up above here.'

He frowned. 'Well get on then, and hurry up to sleep. Won't be no noises to wake you.'

I wondered what he meant, but I just nodded and said goodnight to Annie, who could hardly keep her eyes open. 'You'll be warm in that little truckle bed in the kitchen,' I told her, and smiled as she nodded and disappeared.

My room above the front of the inn was small and had just a bed and a chest beneath the window where I supposed I should keep my clothes. A broken mirror hung on one wall, and there was a faded picture on the opposite wall, a painting of a beach somewhere. I hoped that the sheets and blankets I had found and hung by the fire all afternoon were dry, and quickly got into bed. There were lumps and bumps in the straw mattress, and the one pillow smelt of tobacco smoke. But I was so tired I just curled up and shut my eyes, wondering what tomorrow would bring.

I awoke in the darkness, heart racing.

Horse hooves, rough voices, the jumble of harness and wheels churning up the sand . . . I lay there for a minute. What was happening? I remembered that Ben had said there would be no noises to wake me . . . and had said it in a funny sort of way, as if to say, *don't wake up* . . .

After a couple of minutes my curiosity made me get up, pull my shawl around my shoulders and peer out of the window. It was dark — no sign of dawn yet — but there were a couple of lights down there, moving about and handled by people doing something which I couldn't make out. After a bit I heard the voices rising, talking to each other.

'Henry Winthrop, he said get it all up there before first light. I'll take the cart.'

Another voice, which I suddenly knew was Ben's, replied, 'He said as he'll take another shipment after this one. He's keen to get the old place going, so we need all we can bring in. Get on, then.'

My eyes were getting used to the dark, and in the shifting lantern light I saw a horse and cart loaded with what looked like chests or boxes pull away and head down the lane leading to the road. Then there were horses' hooves approaching, and I made out the shadowy shape of a horse trotting up to the inn, harness jingling as it stopped, and Matthew's gruff voice saying, 'All away safely, Ben, is it?'

The door banged shut, and then all was quiet again. I went back to bed and lay there, thinking. And before I finally slid off to sleep, I understood what had happened out there in the dark of the night.

Smugglers had brought up the latest load of contraband, and it was being taken out in carts and in small boats from the Admiral. Well! Of course I knew that smugglers were about — the whole village knew that they came ashore when the night was dark, and local men carried off the loads of tobacco, tea, snuff, lace and brandy to the people who paid money for them. It was common knowledge, and even the gentry were glad to get their deliveries of cheap stuff. Gossip said that the parish priest drank smuggled brandy, and lots of shopkeepers drank tea, took snuff, and even gave the smuggled lace to their wives to make smart gowns. Because the taxes were high and most of the ordinary people couldn't pay them, the smugglers and their goods were welcome, even helped as they brought the goods ashore and then delivered them to their customers.

When I got up in the morning, I told myself how foolish I had been, not even guessing that the Admiral might be a smuggler's storage place — all those outbuildings and even a derelict cottage. So Ben and Matthew, like their father the old captain, were involved in the free trading. And so was Mr Winthrop. I wondered as I went downstairs, to find Annie stoking the fire, whether I was a smuggler, too, working here. The idea made me smile, and I was still smiling when Master Ben came into the room.

He gave me a very straight look and asked, 'How did you sleep?'

I turned away to put out plates and mugs on the long, scrubbed table and said quietly, 'With a few disturbances. Gets noisy around here, doesn't it? But they didn't worry me, thank you, Master.'

I caught the look in his eyes, which I thought was one of relief. And then he came a step nearer, saying, 'Yes, there's owls in them big trees,' which made me hide my grin. He went on, 'Mr Winthrop is sending his old servant, Mrs Mudge, over to help with the cooking. She lives just up the road. Think he's taken a liking to you, saucy as you are. But I dare say you'll be glad to have some help.'

I turned and gave him a sweet smile. 'That's good, Master. Annie and I can get on with the cleaning then — I'll scrub out the room beside the dairy next.'

He was quick to come nearer then, lowering his voice. 'Just don't touch anything stored in there, see? Valuables, they are.'

I cut slices of green bacon and slid them into the pan on the fire, answering as the fat started to sizzle, 'I won't touch nothing I shouldn't, Master. I'll do just as you say. Will you take an egg with your breakfast?'

There was a lighter note in his voice as he said, 'I'll take two and a slice o' bread. I'm that hungry.' *Yes, I thought, for you were up half the night working.* Our eyes met again and I saw relief shining in his. So we understood one another. He was a smuggler and I wouldn't tell on him. And then I wondered if perhaps the pennies he had mentioned might grow in number as the days went by. That made me smile again.

During the afternoon, as Mrs Mudge napped in her chair by the fire after cooking a good meal for everybody — and yes, she was a really good cook

— Annie and I decided to have some fresh air. Annie was a different girl once we left the Admiral behind us and walked over the fields towards the main road leading back to Ringmore.

'Let's go to the Holy Well,' she said, skipping along beside me. 'Us'll make some wishes and then they'll come true and everything'll be different, won't it, Robyn?'

I smiled at her. 'Perhaps, Annie. But wishes don't always come true, you know — and now I've come to work at the inn with Mrs Mudge, who seems a nice, friendly old lady, surely you'll be happier, won't you? Remember, I won't let Master Ben work you too hard.'

She nodded but her smile had gone, and when we reached the old well, tucked away under a hedge on the border of a field, she started ripping a strip of cotton from her petticoat.

'What's that for?' I asked, and watched as she very carefully knelt down by the well, put her hands into the dark water, and shut her eyes. Her lips were working, and I guessed then that she was making her wish. When she'd finished she got up, tied the piece of cotton to a bush that grew over the well, and bowed three times before looking round at me and giving me a smile of great happiness.

'Just have to wait now,' she said, 'and it'll happen, see if it don't. I'll be off to that lace school before you knows it.'

'Lace school?' I was surprised. Of course I knew the lace school at Ringmore was always busy with young girls learning the trade, but how had Annie heard about it?

She said slowly, 'The housekeeper at the work'us did lace work, and she showed me how to start on it. But then Captain Martin came, wanting an apprentice — and so I come here. But I'd like to make lace . . . ' Her small voice was wistful and I felt something move inside me. If I could help her to make the wish come true, then I would. But how?

Horses' hooves sounded on the road

beyond the hedge, then stopped. The next thing I saw was a large arm clad in a blue coat pushing through the brambles, and a man looking at me. A big man with heavy shoulders, dressed in that smart blue coat, wearing a good hat on his well-covered dark hair which curled behind his ears. A man staring at me and speaking in a quiet, deep, musical voice, saying, 'Good day. I think I'm a bit lost — am I anywhere near the Admiral Inn?'

Something happened inside me then. I found myself wishing I could speak like this man did: easily, with a voice like honey pouring from a jar. I wished that my hair wasn't carroty red, and frizzy with the dampness coming off the river; that my shabby dress was new and lovely, and that he would admire it. Oh, how I wished that I looked like a really pretty girl who he might think worthy of talking to, and even getting to know . . .

I said nothing, but simply stared into his deep sea-green eyes and thought how proud his nose was, and how handsome his figure was on the bay horse. It was only when I heard Annie's whisper beside me — 'Robyn, you must answer him' — that I came to my senses, gasped in a deep breath, and said, 'Yes, just go up this lane till you meet another one turning right, and then down towards the river, and the inn is there.'

'Thank you,' he said, bowing slightly and giving me a wonderful smile. We looked at each other for what seemed a never-ending moment but could only have been a few seconds, although I wanted it to go on and on. Then he said, 'Do you live around here? You seem to know the place well,' and I came to again.

I said, 'I work at the Admiral Inn with Annie here. We're just out for a bit of fresh air after a busy morning's work. We're — ' I stopped, for what would he think of me, saying this? A foolish girl full of fancies? But I had to go on. He had to know something about me.

'We're making our wishes here at the Holy Well. Annie has made an offering token to the Lady of the Well, and I will be doing the same.'

I saw a smile fill his lean, handsome face. 'And what will your offering be, I wonder?'

I didn't know what to say next. I couldn't pull up my skirt like Annie had done and tear a strip off my petticoat, could I? I blushed, lowered my head, wished I could learn to control my tongue, and mumbled, 'I don't know . . . '

And then, into the silence building between us, I heard him chuckle, then say, 'Perhaps I can find something for you — here's an apple which I was going to eat with my dinner. Better that you should give it to the Holy Well to further your wishes, I'm sure.' He held out a small reddish apple and I took it in my hand, not knowing what to do next.

Beside me Annie whispered, 'That's a good thing to offer — better than my bit of petticoat. Put it in the water, Robyn.'

He heard her whisper, and as I leaned forward, going down on my knees by the well, I saw him dismount from his horse and kneel beside me. He said, with a big smile, 'My apple but your offering, so we'll do it between us, shall we? I won't ask what your wish is, but I hope it'll come true for you.'

I was too surprised to speak. I saw him put the apple into the dark water, and so I did the same. And our hands touched before we withdrew them. His were warm, and so strong, and I hoped he didn't notice how red mine were from all the washing of the pots in hot soda water.

As we got up, Annie prodded me. 'Now stick the apple on the bush,' she said. 'Find a good twig — yes, that's right.'

I looked at the big man again and he was still smiling. He mounted his horse and then asked, 'May know your name? Robyn, is it? Mine is Daniel

Winters; I'm the new preventive officer in the local customs service down at Ringmore.'

I nearly fainted. Daniel Winters, one of the rough men Ben had warned me about, and he was a customs man! His job was to find smugglers and send them to prison. We had shared an offering to the Holy Well — so whatever might happen next? And would I ever see him again? Oh, I hoped so!

4

He rode away, but with a backward glance and a warm smile. Annie and I walked slowly down the lane behind him, watching until he disappeared around the corner. Only then did I sigh out the last deep breath I'd been holding as dreams and wishes raged around my mind.

I looked down at Annie walking at my side, looking at me curiously, until I said, 'Well, how long do wishes take to come true, Annie? Do you know?'

She laughed her little bell-like laugh and pressed my hand. 'You gotta have patience, Robyn. Maybe a few days, maybe much longer. But they'll all be there one day, you'll see.'

I nodded, but without much hope. Wishes coming true were really only for small children, not for a young woman like me who wanted so much: a man like that charming and friendly Daniel Winters, and a life full of love and satisfaction. Well, I supposed I could only wait. And in the meantime there was work waiting for us back at the Admiral.

Ben was waiting in the tap room, sitting by the fire with a tankard of ale and talking to Matthew. He looked up as we came in at the door, then stood up and frowned across at me. 'Who said you could go out? There's work waiting to be done and that's what you'll be paid fer at the weekend.'

I stood still and watched Annie run into the kitchen. Then I looked at him. 'I've been working hard this morning, and last night, and yesterday morning — and I'll go on working, but I won't be spoken to like that.'

I saw his face tighten and heard his voice grow hard. 'I'll speak as I want — and you, Robyn Lee, remember you're here to work and not to grumble.' He glared at me and I frowned back. But I knew what I had to say.

'I won't grumble, Master, but you must let me have some time off from all the hard work I'm going to be doing. Just an hour in the afternoon, please.'

Matthew Martin, shorter than Ben, and with a face that was always full of disapproval, put his empty tankard on the counter behind him, grunted and stared at me. Clearly he had no time for the new maid in the taproom. He muttered something about women being useless and then walked out of the room, leaving Ben looking at me as if he agreed with those rude words. Watching him, I saw his mouth tighten, but after a few seconds he nodded grudgingly. 'Just an hour then, cos I can see you're a good worker.'

I decided to be really grateful. 'Thank you, Master,' I said, smiling broadly. 'One last favour, as you're being so kind — Annie can have an hour off with me. That's all right then, isn't it?'

I saw surprise ease his face, but I kept my smile going, and after a bit he nodded and gave me a half-grin as he said, 'I suppose so. But you'll have to make up the time — and so I'll need your help tonight. Just be ready after the taproom empties, and I'll tell you what you gotta do. Understand, Robyn Lee?'

Surprise stopped me smiling, but I sensed something exciting about to happen and so I said quickly, 'Yes, Master, I'll be ready.'

He looked pleased and marched out of the room whistling a tune. I guessed that an adventure was on the way, but also knew in the back of my mind that it was probably something to do with his smuggling business.

* * *

The evening was busy, with a crowd of men from the farms around drinking, smoking and telling yarns. Rough voices . . . bawdy laughter . . . tobacco-scented smoke making my eyes sting, but at last the taproom empted and I saw Ben pulling on his jacket and salt-stained old hat. He looked across the room at me and gestured towards the door, and I knew I must get myself ready for whatever he was planning to do. I saw Annie carrying a great tray of empty tankards towards the sink in the kitchen, and called out to her.

'Go to bed, Annie — I'll be there before long. Just have to do something first.' I watched the girl nod and gratefully disappear from sight.

So this was it: the adventure! I ran upstairs and found a thick shawl to tie around my shoulders and an old felt hat to pull down over my knotted hair. It would be damp as the night drew in.

Outside the inn, now that the men drinking there had tramped their separate ways home, it was quiet, with only the regular song of the river sounding in my ears. I waited for Ben to tell me what to do and was amazed when he appeared from the stables behind the inn, leading two horses. 'This is yours,' he said, giving me the reins of a chestnut mare with a white blaze on its nose. 'Hope you can ride?'

I sucked in a long breath. I had never been on a horse before. 'Sort of,' I said bravely, and I saw Ben grin.

'Lady's old and quiet. Just keep her on a tight rein and you'll be all right. We shan't be galloping anywhere — well, you won't.'

He led the two horses to the mounting block and watched while I clumsily climbed onto Lady's broad, warm back, gathering the reins and hoping that I would manage to stay on. Ben mounted, and then I realized that both horses were laden with small barrels. They hung down around the hairy bodies and, in the dark, could hardly be seen. I put down a hand and felt the round shapes of hard wood as they shifted about once Lady began walking out of the yard. And then I knew what this adventure was all about. Ben and I were delivering goods smuggled ashore in the last few nights.

We rounded the inn, hooves crisp on

the dry sand and stubby growth of weeds growing high on the foreshore. The river song grew louder, and then suddenly we were at its side, water beginning to splash around us. I was amazed at all this; Ben was already taking his mount into the water, looking down carefully at the surging river as if finding his way across.

Then I remembered a story I'd heard somewhere in the village — that at low tide in the middle of the summer it was possible to ford the river from the inn to the village of Bishop, directly opposite. I had dismissed this when I heard it — of course one couldn't walk across the mighty river! But now I realized that this was exactly what Ben was doing. And I had to follow.

Ben turned and shouted, 'Keep Lady on a tight rein and just take her where I lead. It's shallow enough tonight.' His voice rose impatiently. 'Come on, Robyn. Not scared, are you?'

Of course I was scared. But could I let Ben know? No,' I shouted back

46

loudly. 'Of course I'm not. I'll follow you.'

He nodded, and I could just make out his grin through the darkness. 'Well, hurry up — Matt's waiting to come on behind you.'

Very carefully I half-turned and saw, standing on the foreshore and waiting to cross the river, a horse and cart. So that was where Matt had been all the evening — loading it up with all the shadowy sacks and tubs I could just make out. This was indeed a big delivery we were making.

Halfway across the river I felt a current flowing strongly against Lady's back. It swept up my legs, soaking my skirt, and I had to put one hand on the horse's mane to keep my balance as well as hold the reins. I thought a wind was blowing up, increasing the strength of the flowing water, and I guessed that this was a sign of the tide turning. Any minute now the river would start to make its way back towards the estuary, and the sea. It would get deeper, stronger, and I knew we had to come back the same way once the smuggled goods had been offloaded. My fright rose, but I knew I could only go on.

I was thankful when once again Lady's legs rose out of the water and started to scrape against sand and pebbles on the opposite shore. We had arrived safely! Ben had halted just ahead of me and was looking back anxiously at the horse and cart Matt was struggling to bring across the river. When at last the cart wheels pushed onto the foreshore and the horse pulled strongly up the slope leading to the river road running close by, he said, 'That's good. Always a bit dangerous, but we've got here. So now there's only one stop for you, Robyn Lee, and then you can go back to the inn. Ride down to the first farm you come to and shout for George Heywood. He'll be waiting to take all your barrels. Then make your way back, quick as you can. Matt and I have further to go. Then we'll come back round the road and through the village, cos the tide'll be full and we couldn't risk another crossing here. We'll be back at the inn for breakfast. And make sure you have it ready . . . '

He rode off into the engulfing darkness, followed by the creaking and unwieldy cart, with Matt urging the horse on, and I realised I was alone. The river surged menacingly beside me and a sneaky wind was blowing the bits of hair not covered by my hat. I felt a sudden awful sense of real fright — I wanted to be back at the inn, safe in my lumpy bed, with a hot brick at my feet to warm my chilled, wet body. But I knew I had a job to do, and I wouldn't let Ben down, so I said out loud, 'Come on then, Lady — let's go and find that farm.'

Her ears pricked and, as if she knew the way, she turned and walked quietly along the river path. Very soon I saw a light swinging to and fro, guiding me on. This must be George Heywood, waiting to take the delivery of the contraband which I carried.

What a relief to know I only had to help offload the small barrels, and then I could make my way back to the inn. Somehow I pushed aside the fearful thought of the river crossing and said cheerfully to the man who held the lantern and put his hand on Lady's bridle, leading her into a small, shadowy yard, 'Here I am, Mr Heywood. I'll help unload the barrels.' I slid off Lady's back, glad to feel firm earth under my feet once more.

I couldn't see much of him; just an old, leathery face beneath an equally old, battered hat, but his voice was warm. 'Well, 'tis a maid! I thought it would be Ben or Matt or one of Mr Winthrop's men. But you've got the goods, and that's all that matters. Tie up the horse, maid, and us'll start offloading.'

We carried barrels into a shed behind his farmhouse, covering them with old blankets and then putting logs on top of the pile so that no one would know what was underneath. The work helped dry my damp legs and arms and I was warm by the time we'd hidden the last barrel. Then George Heywood said, 'Come in an' have a drink to warm you up afore you go back across the river again,' and although I was glad to accept his invitation, my fears began to build.

And as we sat by a glowing fire, drinking a tot of watered-down rum which he said would help me get home, George said something else which made shivers run down my spine.

'Customs men on patrol tonight, so keep yer eyes open and make sure you don't run into one.'

I stared at him. 'But I can't see in the dark . . . How shall I know if anyone's about?'

'You can't. Just keep going and get back to the inn fast as you can, and bolt the door when you get there. They're keen on searching inns for smuggled goods, so just keep quiet and let 'em go away again.'

I was glad of the warm, optimistic

effect of the small tot of rum which I had swallowed. The night seemed to be getting even more dangerous than I had thought it might be, and my nervousness returned. I thanked him for his kindness, pulled my hat closer over my hair, mounted Lady and trusted her to take the path back to the place where we had crossed from the inn. The good old horse did so without any mishap, and slowly walked along the rough track with me clinging to the reins with one hand and the other grasping her thick mane.

I thought of what George Heywood had said and looked over my shoulder nervously, thinking about customs men, but saw nothing and heard only the roar of the rising water.

Suddenly I remembered Ben warning me about rough men, and — oh yes, Daniel Winters, he had said. Even as Lady took me nearer and nearer to the frightening waters, my mind spun off in a different direction, taking me to that warm, sunny afternoon when Daniel and I had made our wish in the Holy Well. No, I couldn't believe that Daniel, with his warm smile and heart-stopping handsome face, was one of the rough men . . .

But then, abruptly, I forgot that dreamy afternoon, for I heard the noise of the rising waters close at hand. Already Lady had slowed down and turned, facing the river; and I knew, shivering, that we were about to make the crossing. I tightened my grip on the reins, tucked my knees closer to her warm, hairy body, and closed my eyes as Lady slowly made her way into the surging water.

5

Yes, the river was stronger and more threatening now. I guessed the tide had turned, and a cold wind blew relentlessly as we slowly made our way across. I was just thinking how lucky we were to have nearly made it to the far side, when a sudden squall of wind and wave came rushing down, hitting Lady with a force that made her stagger, and in that fearsome moment I felt myself slipping. The reins fell out of my hands and I was spread-eagled across Lady's strong back. Only by desperately pulling myself up straight again, did I manage not to fall off into the surging waters.

I had never been so scared. The darkness, the wind whistling its threats in my ears, the force and the rising voice of the river all around me were so frightening that all I could do was shout to Lady, 'Go on! Go on, we've got to get home . . . ' And bless her, she did so. Somehow she found her stride again and ploughed on through the waves.

Oh, what relief to feel her feet firm on the foreshore again, and to know I was safe. The cold, soaked skirts and wet feet didn't matter any longer. I was alive — and all thanks to that dear old horse. I was smiling again as we jogged along, away from the river and into the yard, where I slid off Lady's back and took her into the stable. I made sure she had a good supply of hay, and with a rug I found gave her a quick rub-down before making my shivering way back to the inn. I bolted the door behind me, wearily climbed the stairs and then found that dear Annie had put a warm brick in my bed.

It was only as I took off my damp clothes and combed out my tangled wet curls that I discovered my shawl was missing. I guessed it had become untied and fallen off when Lady struggled with the rising river. By now it would have been washed away. A pity, but rather the shawl than me, I thought as thankfully I climbed into my warm bed and closed my eyes.

The morning came all too soon. The pale dawn light aroused me, along with a noisy cockerel at the farm down the road, and I knew I must get down to the kitchen and fire up the hearth ready for the breakfast Ben and Matthew would soon be expecting. Mrs Mudge wouldn't be here this early, so it was up to me and Annie to do the best we could.

Annie, pushing her truckle bed into a far corner of the kitchen, smiled at me as she quickly dressed and tidied her hair into her cap. 'So you didn't get washed away, then?'

I felt my smile fade as my thoughts returned to that awful, frightening ride through the surging waters. But I pushed them away and said lightly, 'Not me, but my shawl was. I don't suppose I'll see it again.'

There were noises out in the yard

and I ran to the door. The Martin brothers had come home, Matt with the cart and Ben on his grey horse. They looked as if the night had been a long one, and I couldn't help calling out, 'Come in — the fire's burning and I'll cook you some breakfast.'

Matt took no notice. He untacked the old cart horse from the shafts and led it into the stables, coming back in a few seconds for Ben's mount and then disappearing again. Ben came towards me as I waited at the door and suddenly put an arm around my shoulders, pulling me close. 'You're a good maid. You did well,' he said, and unexpectedly bent his head and kissed me.

Well! I was so surprised that I did nothing. I simply waited until he stepped back, grinning, and then I said what was flashing through my shocked mind. 'What did you do that for?'

'Cos you're a good maid, and you did well last night. You deserve a reward.'

'And a kiss is all I get?'

His grin faded. 'So what else do you

want? Girls, always wanting some-thing . . . '

I turned back into the kitchen. 'No, no, I'm not like that, Master. I'd just like my shawl to come back. It got washed away when Lady stumbled on the way home.'

He followed me inside and sank down heavily in the big captain's chair by the fire, throwing his hat onto the floor and stretching out his legs. 'You won't see that again, maid. Swept out to sea with the tide, I reckon. But I might give you something else one day. Perhaps.'

I cracked eggs into the pan and looked at him. Teasingly, I asked, 'Is that a promise, Master?'

'Call me Ben. 'tis more friendly.' His voice was warmer, and I wondered at the change in his attitude. A kiss, and now wanting to be my friend? Well, better than always being at odds with him, I supposed. I put his breakfast on a plate and slid it along the table towards him.

Then I remembered poor old Matt outside in the stable. 'Shall I cook something for Matt, too?' I asked.

He said, with his mouth full, 'Don't fuss 'bout him. He's that slow always. If he's hungry he'll tell you so.'

I stared. Hardly the way someone should feel about his brother, I thought. He added, 'Dunno why we keep on together — I'm the one who does all the hard work.' Then, swallowing the last mouthful of egg and bacon, he added, 'What about a drink to help me dry out? Something hot. Here's the key to the tea caddy — up there, see? Make a brew, maid.'

I said nothing, but thought all the more. Clearly Master Ben was in charge of whatever was going on here at the Admiral, and his brother Matt was just his grumpy servant. I felt a pang of sympathy for the poor man, but then the key to the caddy was in my hand and I glanced back at Annie as I reached up to the mantle. We grinned briefly at each other, and I was glad that her fear of the terrible Master was plainly growing less. It was a good thing I had come here to take up this situation. My ever-curious mind drifted off to the future, when with Ben's more friendly ways, I might suggest I took over all the keys and really manage the household and everything in it — yes, even the smuggled goods outside in the sheds and outhouses. As I made a huge pot of tea, I smiled to myself. How very exciting life had suddenly become.

The door swung open and Matt came in, anxiety written all over his plain face and fear in his raised, hoarse voice. 'Customs men just coming down the lane. A whole troop of them. What'll us do, Ben?'

For a stretching moment there was silence in the kitchen, broken only by deep intakes of breath. Annie stared at me. I watched while Ben slowly got to his feet, turned and looked at his brother. No one spoke until Ben turned again, looking at me, the expression on his face one that alarmed me. Slowly, he said, 'You better go, maid, an' tell the preventive men that we ain't here, Matt an' me. Not back from our fishing last night, say. That'll shut 'em up, with any luck. Cor — ' He swiveled round and spoke to Matt in a rapid, breathy voice. ' — we don't want 'em looking at our accounts — that's what they'll want, I reckon. I've heard say that this new man is a devil for accounts. So let's get out the back way, and hide ourselves till they're gone.'

Listening and watching, with a stab of alarm, I said quickly, 'But don't leave me to deal with them, Master. I don't know nothing 'bout customs men and accounts . . .'

Ben, halfway through the door that led to a small passage hidden from the view of the kitchen, called back, 'Course you can do it. Just make 'em laugh, like you do with me. Say we won't be back from fishing for a while, and then they'll leave us alone. You'll do it proper, Robyn, maid.' With those words he and Matt disappeared, the

61

door slammed shut, and I realised I was left with a very difficult matter to resolve on my own.

Annoyance mingled with pride. After all, not everyone would be trusted to act for their master, would they? But then I found myself wondering, what if the customs men didn't believe what I told them? Or, worse still, didn't laugh at me — what then?

Annie came to my side, whispering, 'They won't take us away, will they, Robyn? I don't want to go to gaol.'

That did it. At the mere idea of being imprisoned, my energy arose. No gaol for us; certainly not. I could deal with these wretched customs men. Like Ben said, I would face them and make them leave.

I put a hand on Annie's shoulder. 'Get on with your work, Annie, and stop worrying. They can't hurt us. I won't let them.'

Suddenly there was a loud knock at the door. I stood up straighter, tidied a few errant curls back under my cap, and marched out of the kitchen, through the empty taproom, and down the shadowy passage. Then I reached out with determined hands to pull back the iron bar holding the door shut.

It opened with its usual groan and squeak, and I found myself looking straight into the piercing eyes of Daniel Winters. He stood there, clearly the man in charge of the small troop of mounted preventive men that accompanied him. 'Good day,' he said, and his voice was far from friendly. 'Are Ben and Matthew Martin here? I need to see them.'

For a long moment I was speechless. So this lovely man, who had been so warm and pleasant only the other day, was really a preventive officer in search of smugglers. Of course he was. I took in the deep blue coat and the tall hat held in strong hands at his side. But I hadn't known, that lovely afternoon by the Holy Well, when I had thought him just a stranger looking for somewhere particular in a land he didn't know too well.

A customs man — the very person I would never want to see on the doorstep of the inn. Did he know the brothers were smugglers? My mind raced. And I was a smuggler, too — so whatever would this stern-looking Daniel Winters say about that?

I struggled to find words. Make him laugh, said Ben. Laugh? What could I say? Then I recalled my orders, and unsteadily said, 'Ben and Matt are still away. Fishing last night, you see.' Well, it wasn't really a lie. It was just that they were dealing with the results of a particular sort of fishing, wasn't it? I looked again into those deep eyes and added, 'Can you come back another day, when they're here?'

'No.' The one word was heavy and I felt my heart start to race. 'If you work here,' Daniel Winters went on, 'you'll know where the accounts are kept. You can show them to me. I haven't come all this way for nothing, you know.'

I felt that that lovely meeting at the

Holy Well had been a dream. And this was a nightmare. Make him laugh — somehow I must do so. I wondered wildly whether I could ask if this was my wish coming true, but that wasn't really funny.

And then the answer came. For out of one deep coat pocket hung something I recognised.

It was easy, then, to smile broadly, point at his pocket, and say lightly, 'Why, you've found my shawl! All wet and bedraggled it must be. I dropped it by the riverside and I suppose it got washed away. Wherever did you find it?' I gave him no chance to reply, adding brightly, 'How nice of you to come and give it back to me. I'm so grateful, Mr Winters.' I watched his face ease out of its stern expression as he kept looking at me, and so smiled again, saying, 'Perhaps you might come in and have a drink? I've got the fire going, and a brew of tea would warm you up . . . '

But he said, with a hard note in his deep, low voice, 'That's kind of you,

Miss Lee. And while I'm drinking your tea and perhaps looking at the accounts, you can tell me what were you doing at the riverside last night? Why did you need to cross the river? You must have done, for I found this shawl on the bank just below the old crossing. Got your feet wet in the water, did you? But you're a bright maid, so I expect you'll have a reason for it — and now, shall we go in and look for those accounts?'

6

It was hard to know what to say, or even whether to go on smiling at him, or frown. I felt in a real muddle so just stood there while he stepped into the passage, forcing me to walk back into the kitchen. Annie stood in the far corner, her eyes wide, for obviously she had heard what this preventive officer had said. I thought that in a moment she would disappear and hide, which was actually what I would have liked to do, but oh no. Ben had given me orders — had said I could manage without him — and I was determined to do so.

As we walked into the kitchen my mind was busy trying to work out plans which would keep this nosy customs man from finding anything which might bring punishment to all of us at the inn. How to do it? And then I knew. I had boasted that I would make the old

Admiral look clean and attractive. Here was my chance to start on the idea.

I made a pot of tea while Daniel Winters looked around the room and even started moving furniture — he was pushing his hand behind the big dresser, I supposed to see if there was anything hidden there. Then he stretched up to the shelf where we kept the pots and pans and ran his fingers in between the things standing there. As I poured and then pushed a mug across the table towards him, I said brightly, 'There you are, Mr Winters. When you've drunk that I'll take you over the inn. Of course I haven't gone very far with my plan yet, but we're slowly getting there.' I looked at him over the rim of my mug and saw surprise spread over his handsome face.

He drank some tea, put down the mug and looked at me very curiously. 'And what exactly is this plan of yours, Miss Lee?'

'Why, to give the old Admiral a new look — cleaned up, freshly painted, new furniture perhaps, and attractive enough to bring lots of people here.' I paused, for he frowned now, as if I was talking nonsense. So I added very firmly, 'And I have Ben's approval. Mr Winthrop, when he was here, said it was a good idea too. You know him, I expect? A gentleman, living just up the road in a beautiful old house.'

'Yes,' Daniel Winters said, and I guessed from his tone that he had suspicions about Mr Winthrop as well as the two Martin brothers.

Hastily, I put down my tea mug and moved towards the door. 'Please come with me, Mr Winters, and I'll show you how far we've got with my plan. Now the kitchen of course, has already been cleaned, and made much easier to work in . . . and the taproom is looking so much better. Come and see it.' I walked down the passage and into the tap-room, glad that the sun shone through the windows and made it all look rather attractive.

But clearly Daniel Winters didn't

want to do as I suggested. He stayed where he was, in the kitchen doorway, and said very firmly, 'Miss Lee, all I need to see are Ben Martin's accounts. So please take me to wherever they might be. I haven't got all day, you know.'

I turned and gave him my best smile. 'Oh, where are you going next? I suppose being a customs man keeps you very busy. But I was hoping we might meet again one afternoon by the Holy Well, and I could show you some more lovely places that you would enjoy seeing.'

He looked very strange, and I wondered if I had gone too far. But then I saw a hint of amusement lift his lovely straight lips, and I said quietly, 'Of course, that's very forward of me. I don't expect you have time to meet anyone when you should be working, do you?'

He stood beside me, and I saw a proper smile warm his face. 'Miss Lee, you are very persuasive. Shall we make a bargain? If you show me the room where the accounts are kept, I will try and find an hour or two one afternoon when we can explore the countryside. Tell me, where do you intend to take me next time we meet?'

'Oh, the tunnel,' I said without thinking. And then I bit my lip, for of course that was a smuggling tunnel, cut out of the cliff on Ness Beach to allow contraband goods an easy way into the village, where the goods would be delivered. I tried to cover up my stupid mistake, saying quickly, 'But that's a long way from here. I'm sure we could find somewhere much nearer that you would enjoy visiting . . . '

He laughed — actually laughed — and then said, 'Let's get the accounts looked at, and then we'll make our arrangements to meet in a day or two.'

So we really would meet again! And perhaps he would forget then that he was a customs officer. But then my mind jumped. Even meeting Daniel Winters again and wandering around the countryside in the sunshine wouldn't change the fact that I was a smuggler, would it?

I was wondering how I could get him safely past the little side room where I thought Ben kept all his papers, but then footsteps sounded along the passage and Mrs Mudge appeared. She stopped and stared at me and then at Daniel Winters. After a moment, in which surprise spread all over her lined face, she said, 'What's he doing here? We don't want customs men coming in and telling us what to do. Real nasty men, they are. You, Robyn — show this man the door, and then we'll get on with cooking the dinner.' She hobbled into the kitchen and Daniel and I were left looking at each other.

'She's not usually so bad-tempered,' I hurried to say, 'but perhaps her legs hurt. She was complaining about them yesterday. And oh, Mr Winters, before you go you really must come up and see the wonderful room at the top of the house where I can imagine all the new visitors enjoying themselves. It's this way, up these stairs. They're very dark, Mr Winters, so mind you don't trip.'

I was halfway up the staircase when I heard his voice below in the passage — not his usual quiet, pleasant voice, but quick, hard words with a bit of a growl in them. 'Just show me the accounts, girl — I haven't got time to wander about like this.'

I turned at the top of the stairs, wondering how on earth I could stop him from seeing those wretched accounts. I held my breath for a few seconds and then made myself say quietly, as if I had no worries at all, 'I will, Mr Winters, but you really must come and see this room first. Please?'

Through the shadows I saw his face looking up at me, and I was thinking that maybe he really would come up, when Annie came running down the corridor ahead of me. Her small voice was raised as she shouted, 'I found this. It's horrible!'

I stared. She was holding a huge,

shiny brown pistol with iron fittings, and a deadly look about it. I gasped. 'Annie! Where did you get that? Put it down, quick . . . '

But she held on to it, and my heart jumped as I saw it was pointed at Daniel Winters. 'I found it on a chair in one of the bedrooms,' she said in her tiny, high voice. 'I think it belongs to Master Ben. I've seen him with it . . . '

Daniel came rushing up the stairs. He pushed me aside, grabbed the weapon from Annie's shaking hands, and put it in his belt. 'Downstairs with you both at once. No more playing about. That's it, quickly now..'

We went slipping down the stairs as if in fear of our lives. Where had that nice man gone, I wondered as I came to a halt in the passage, looking up at him as he followed us down.

He was very angry, with a hard mouth and a stern gleam in his beautiful eyes. 'I fear I'm a man of the law,' he said tightly, coming to my side and looking down at me. 'And so you must do as I say, or it'll be the worse for you.'

We stared at each other, and I thought that after all my dreams, Mr Winters had become my foe and was no longer my friend.

His voice cut into my thoughts. 'And, Miss Lee, this time you will show me the room where Martin keeps his accounts. Yes, now . . . this minute, if you please.'

What could I do but take him to the room that Ben kept locked, and then wait while he tried to open the door? 'He locks it,' I said feebly, and Daniel looked at me as if I were an idiot.

'Yes,' he said, but his one word was fierce. Then he added, 'Stand aside, girls.'

We stepped away and watched while he put his shoulder to the door. The first blow merely made the wood creak, but the next one forced the lock and the door flew open.

He went inside, looked around, and made straight away for the table in the corner which was littered with papers, books, tobacco pots, dirty mugs and goodness knew what else. He grabbed the big red covered book lying in the middle of all that rubbish and opened it.

'Ah,' he said, and I saw his smile return. But it was not a friendly smile now; more an expression of stern pleasure. 'Got you, Ben Martin,' he said quietly. He closed the book and put it inside his jacket, then turned, looked at Annie and me, and nodded his head.

'Thank you for your help, Miss Lee. I'll take this back to the customs office. We'll have a good look at it.'

His smile warmed and suddenly his hand went into his jacket pocket, where my shawl still hung. He took it out, folded it neatly, and then gave it me. Now his face was grave, but I thought I heard a hint of warmth in the low, deep voice. 'Keep this safe, Robyn, and don't go out at night again.' His sea-green eyes looked deep into mine. 'I'm warning you.' And then he turned and was gone.

Annie and I heard the door creak and slam as he left, and voices among the men he'd left waiting outside. Then horses' hooves trotting away, and finally just the faint song of the river and the calls of gulls sweeping over the water.

We looked at each other but could think of nothing sensible to say, so we went back to the kitchen and offered to help Mrs Mudge cook the dinner. I knew we were thinking all the more as we scraped vegetables and washed dishes. Daniel Winters had made a huge impression on both of us.

7

I helped clear away the dinner plates, hoping that Ben, who had come back during the morning, wouldn't go on shouting at me for letting the customs man see his accounts book. He'd been very angry. 'I told you not to let him in that room, you stupid maid — what did you do that for?'

I told him I couldn't stop Mr Winters knocking the door in and then taking the book. 'Don't blame me, Master. Why weren't you here to stop him yourself?'

He growled something I couldn't make out, went past me with a slap to my shoulder, and then turned at the door, gave me a glare and said, 'Saucy maid! Just keep outta my way, d'you hear?' And he was gone.

I hung up the dish cloth and looked at Mrs Mudge, who shook her head.

Then I went to find Annie in the scullery with the never-ending pots. 'Come on,' I said. 'We're going out. Can't stand no more of his bad temper. Leave those old pots and get your shawl.'

Annie's smile was bright enough to make me give her one back. 'Where'll we go?' she asked.

I said at once, without thinking, 'To tell Mr Winthrop about the accounts book and Master Ben being so cross. I don't have to put up with all his nastiness.'

Mrs Mudge, putting her feet up on a stool in front of the fire, called a last order: 'Be back in time to open the taproom when all the men come, you maids.'

I didn't answer; just grinned at Annie and settled my straw hat firmly on my head. 'Come on,' I said, and she didn't need any more persuasion.

Outside it was sunshine and a mischievous warm wind that blew our skirts about as we walked down the lane and turned into the road leading to Mr Winthrop's big house. I pushed away all the business of this morning — of Mr Winters being so hard on me and taking the accounts book, and saying, 'I've got you, Ben Martin,' with a gleam in his eyes, so that I thought it sounded like a sentence to go to gaol. So Ben hadn't paid his taxes — was that it? But Daniel — yes, this afternoon, in the sunny countryside, he had become Daniel in my easier mind — hadn't said anything about smuggling. But then, that pistol Annie had found — surely that proved that Ben could be a rough, even violent man. As we walked, I pushed aside all the confusing questions and thought instead how lucky Annie and I were to be out here. I heard larks singing high up in the blue, blue sky, wild flowers budded in the hedges, and Annie bent to pick the first pale primroses bordering the road.

'I'll put 'em in a little pot and smell 'em all day,' she said, grinning at me.

When we reached Mr Winthrop's big

iron gate we looked at each other, and our smiles faded. What would he say, seeing us here?

'Must we go in?' asked Annie with a scared look.

I shrugged my shoulders bravely. 'Of course. He's got to know about Master Ben being nasty to us.'

Annie's eyes opened wider than usual. 'But what if he's nasty, too?'

I took her hand and we walked up the gravel path towards the huge front door where a brass horse's head knocker glinted at us. 'If he is, then we'll run down to Ringmore and have a cup of tea with my mother. Come on.' I struck a blow with the horse's head and heard it echo through the house. Then — silence. We looked at each other and even my smile disappeared.

There were footsteps at last and the door opened. An elderly maid wearing a black dress and lovely white streamers on her cap looked disapprovingly at us. 'And what might you be wanting?' she asked, and added before I could reply,

'It would be better if you'd gone round to the servants' entrance.'

That annoyed me and gave me fresh strength. I pulled my shoulders back and said quietly, but with a very firm voice, 'We wish to see Mr Winthrop. Please tell him Miss Lee and Miss Annie are here, from the Admiral. And I have news for him.'

The maid looked as if an angel from heaven had smote her. Her eyes were wide and her mouth open, but she stepped backwards and her voice quavered as she said, 'Come in then, if you please, miss. Take a seat here in the hall and I'll ask if the master is free to see you.'

I thanked her and sat down in one of the ornate chairs lining the space all around us. I nodded at Annie and she sat nervously on the very edge of her seat. We looked at one another, but said nothing.

A door opened at the far end of the hall and Mr Winthrop appeared. He came to where we sat, gave me a slight, curious smile, and asked, 'What can I do for you, Miss Lee? And little Miss Annie of the pots?'

I stood up, my heart jumping, and couldn't think how to answer. It was Annie who came to the rescue. 'I found a pistol, sir, and it belongs to Master Ben. And the customs man has smashed down the door and taken Master's book. Master's very angry with us, and we don't know what to do about it.'

I felt my mouth drop open. Little Annie, talking so much! But it gave me new confidence, and so I added my own part of the story. 'Master Ben hid when the customs man and his patrol came, and we couldn't stop him — Mr Winters — from getting into the room where the accounts book was kept. He's taken it back to Ringmore, to the customs people, and the magistrate. Do you think they'll put Master Ben in gaol, sir? Because if so, we won't have our jobs anymore, and what'll we do then?'

'Hmmm,' said Mr Winthrop, pulling his mouth into a sort of frown, though he still looked at me kindly. 'I think we'd better go into my study and have a talk about all this, Miss Lee.' He gestured with his arm towards a closed door at the other side of the hall, and Annie and I walked in front of him. Opening the door, he said, 'Please sit down, both of you, while I think what to do.'

We found chairs and sat, and I watched him as he went around the big leather-topped desk to his own chair, sank into it and put his elbows on the desk, hands steepled in front of his face. 'Ben Martin with a pistol, eh? I can believe that. And not paying his taxes — yes, that too. What a fool the man is. I suppose I shall have to get him out of it yet again.' His voice was quiet and slow, as if talking to himself. But then he looked at me across the desk and I saw his expression become more serious, with lines stretching from nose to mouth, making him look older.

'You don't want to lose your positions, Miss Lee, Miss Annie?' he asked, and we shook our heads. 'Well then, I think I must explain things to you. You see . . . ' He sat back in his chair and clasped his hands in front of himself on the desk. Black eyes stared into mine. 'You are a bright girl, Miss Lee, and I understand from Ben that you work well for him. Even to the point of running errands at night . . . ' Here he stopped and a frown spread over his face. 'I believe you made the river crossing with him yesterday. Brave of you, and I hope you understood exactly what you were doing?'

I took a deep breath. I felt nervous because of his serious look, but I knew I must answer honestly. 'Yes, Mr Winthrop. I carried small barrels on the horse and delivered them to the Greenslade farm lower down the river. It was difficult coming back, for the horse slipped and I was very afraid, but I managed to stay on, thank goodness.'

'Yes.' He was still looking at me with

that hard expression.

I swallowed the lump forming in my throat, as I knew that I had to ask him the important question. 'Was it . . . smuggling, Mr Winthrop?' I heard the fright in my voice, but I kept looking at him.

Again he said, 'Yes, it was, Miss Lee. And because of that night-time ride you are now one of the band of smugglers that Ben and Matthew Martin have gathered around them.'

My thoughts ran in circles, but I understood what he was saying. After a moment's silence I gathered enough courage to ask unsteadily, 'Are you one of the band, Mr Winthrop?' Because it was important to know. I didn't want Ben or Matthew to be the leader of the band, if I was still to work for them; but if this gentleman was in charge then I thought I would be treated much better.

I heard Annie, at my side, suck in a huge breath and then noisily let it go. Her hand crept into mine, and I clasped it tightly. Would he tell me the truth? Or would he simply tell me to mind my own business and do whatever Ben asked next?

At last he spoke; his voice was slower, and the expression on his face had eased slightly. He said, 'I am their supervisor, Miss Lee. And yours, too. I do no smuggling, but I help store the contraband and distribute it to my friends around about.' A smile crept over his mouth. 'The parson likes his brandy. Mrs Clifton-Jones at the big house insists on china tea for her parties, and has her gowns trimmed with Brussels lace; while her husband takes snuff, free of tax. Her daughter, Anthea, likes Indian muslins for her summer dresses. You see, free trading is a way of life these days, and no one thinks any the worse of it.'

We sat there in silence, he smiling at me, my thoughts running riot. I couldn't think what to say next, for all that he had told me was surprising and not as wicked as I had feared it would be. So I was a smuggler. And I wasn't really ashamed of it . . .

A new thought struck me and I asked, 'Will the smuggling we do help Master Ben turn the Admiral into a nice new inn, Mr Winthrop?'

Now he got to his feet and started pacing the room. 'Yes, Miss Lee; indeed it will. Captain Martin was an old and dear friend of mine, and I knew of his ambition to improve his inn, so I am doing what I can to help Ben and Matthew make enough money to do this.' He stopped behind my chair and I heard his voice, deep and warm and strangely friendly, as he added, 'I hope this will reassure you that what we are doing with our small amounts of free trading is in no way worryingly criminal; only exactly what other people are doing all over the country.' He stepped slightly away but stood beside my chair, bending and looking at me with those intense dark eyes. 'So what do you say, Miss Lee? Are you one of us, and will you continue to help Ben with his deliveries?'

I said at once, 'Yes, Mr Winthrop. Of course. And thank you for explaining so clearly.'

'Good.' He took my hand and drew me up from the chair. 'And now let me show you a few pleasantries which will help you to understand just what we can do with the good old Admiral. Come this way . . .'

He led us out of his study, along the tiled hallway and into what I thought must be the drawing room. What a room! I stood and gasped, and Annie's fingers dug into mine as we looked around. It was a large room, full of beautiful furniture which shone with polish as the afternoon sun glinted on to it through huge floor-length windows. On the tables and shelves stood ornaments which I couldn't stop looking at: china, silver, ivory carvings . . . And on the wall hung portraits and watercolours which filled my head with images. I stood in the middle of this room, my feet loving the thick, colourful carpet, my eyes running from one wall to the other.

'Well?' said Mr Winthrop, and he was smiling.

'If this is what we can make the Admiral look like, then I'll do anything to help,' I said quickly. 'It's all so beautiful — and how people will love to see the old inn come to life like this wonderful room. Oh, Mr Winthrop, when can we make a start on it, do you think?'

He took my hand, led me to a large floral covered armchair and sat me down on it. Then he went to Annie and took her to the opposite side of the fire, and pulled out a stool. 'Sit here, young lady,' he said. Stepping to the fireside, he pulled a woven bell pull. 'We will have some tea,' he said. When the elderly maid came to the door, he ordered, 'Cream cakes, if you please, Lizzie, and that special tea, for the three of us. At once.'

'Yes, sir,' said the maid. She curtseyed and was gone.

I still had a worry running around my mind. 'But Master Ben, and the accounts book, and that customs man, Mr Winters, and the magistrate — oh sir, what will happen about all that?'

He pulled up a chair, sat down, and stretched out long legs. His smile was untroubled. 'Don't worry, Miss Lee. I shall go down to the customs office, pay stupid Ben's overdue taxes, and give that Mr Winters some exciting information which will take him and his patrol heading off to the other end of the town. Oh yes, it will all settle down, and then we can get to work again.'

We sat there, Annie and I staring at each other, and I guessed she was thinking the same as me: our lives were changing, and oh how exciting it was.

8

After we'd eaten wonderful scones, cream and raspberry jam, and drunk some very strong tea which neither Annie nor I really enjoyed, we thanked Mr Winthrop for everything and then made our way back to the Admiral. He came to the door with us, watched us go down the gravel path and called after us, 'Remember all I have said, Miss Lee. And be very careful as you go about your work. I shall be watching out for you.'

After a few footsteps, Annie said, 'Is he a good man, Robyn, or someone just a bit better than Master Ben? Do you trust him?'

I thought for a moment, watching the birds flying down the river, listening to the sound of the water flowing soft and gentle today, and then said slowly, 'I think Mr Winthrop is a hard man, just doing what he wants to do, but he'll be good to us if we behave ourselves. And he'll make sure that Master Ben doesn't ill-treat us, which is really all that we need worry about.' I looked down at her, saw her eyes widen, and felt her hand slip into mine as she said very quietly, 'I wanted to ask him about the lace school, but I thought he might not like me talking too much.'

'Oh yes, the lace school.' My thoughts went off in a new direction and in a minute I said, 'Well, Annie, I think we must do something about that. You're very young to do all this hard work at the inn. Perhaps we can persuade Master Ben to give you free afternoons and then you can go into Shaldon to the school.'

'Oh, Robyn!' Her face was one huge smile, and I felt a sudden need to do all I could to help her into a better life. As we walked on, I thought about money. I could give a little towards her lessons, and she earned some pennies as well, so perhaps between us . . . And then I had a good idea. Master Ben knew that Annie understood what was going on at the inn; so, if he didn't want her talking out of turn, would he be willing to give her some extra pennies? I would ask him.

We reached the inn, which shone in the late afternoon sun, and behind it the grey-green river flowed like the wind running through a file of corn. I stopped for a moment, thinking how lovely it was here and how I enjoyed this countryside. I was lucky to be here, and hoped I could stay for as long as I wanted. But the smuggling — suppose we were caught out and brought before the magistrate? Would Mr Winthrop be able to get us off without a sentence, either to gaol or transportation to a far-off country? And that made me think of Mr Winters with his stern face when he picked up the accounts book. Yet he had said he might meet me at the Holy Well one afternoon — had he really meant that? And should I, perhaps tomorrow, go along there in the hope of seeing him?

I sighed and pushed open the inn door. We both went inside, into shadows and the smell of ale and tobacco. The lovely fresh afternoon was over, and we were both back at work.

Mrs Mudge waited in the kitchen, her afternoon nap finished, and all the pots and pans on the range put ready to cook an evening meal. She looked up and said, 'Time you were back. Vegetables to clean, Annie; and Robyn, Master Ben's upstairs. Said he didn't want to be disturbed.' Her face tightened. 'Not in a good mood, he isn't, so careful how you go.'

When Annie and I had prepared the vegetables and put plates on the long table, I caught her eye and whispered, while Mrs Mudge's back was turned, 'Come with me.' Very quietly we both crept out of the kitchen, and I headed for the little room where Master Ben had kept his accounts book. I felt curious about it — what else did he keep in it? I wondered.

With Annie at my side I opened the door with its broken lock, and very quietly we went in, closing the door behind us. It was a small room with a table in the centre littered with papers and tobacco bowls and some long emptied glasses, a big wooden chair beside it, and shelves all around two walls full of what looked like ledgers. Annie stared up at them. 'All that writing,' she said, her face aghast. But I was more interested in an old bureau with a carved lid which stood against the far wall by a small window looking out onto the river.

Yes writing, I thought, and numbers in accounts and invoices and receipts perhaps; but there was a portrait hanging over the desk which I found much more interesting. I remembered that Ben had told us this was his father's room, where the captain had sat when he wasn't in the taproom talking to all his old friends and drinking partners. I wished I had known Captain Martin, for people in the village always said he was a gentleman who had gone wrong, and that his two sons were no better than they should be, which I understood. Had the captain been in the smuggling business like they were? Like Mr Winthrop was? I looked around for something to fill in the blanks in my mind. What had Captain Martin been like? And how would I ever find out about him?

'Look.' Annie caught my arm and pointed at the wall above the bureau. 'Who's that, do you think, Robyn?'

I stood quite still and stared. It was a small portrait — an oil painting, I supposed, of a young woman. The frame was dark oak and emphasised her fair hair and her pale blue eyes. Something about that small, pretty face staring into the unseen distance held my gaze for a few moments. Annie, also looking at it, suddenly said wistfully, 'Look at that lace. Isn't it lovely? Wonder if I'll ever make something like that.'

I smiled down at her and said, 'Remember your wish. Maybe it'll come true one day.'

Her smile disappeared as she said, 'Listen! I can hear footsteps coming downstairs. It must be the master! We'd better run, Robyn . . . he won't want to find us here . . . '

I stopped, wondering about the woman in the portrait with the lovely lace collar, and about Captain Martin — about everything except being caught by Ben in his private little room. I grabbed Annie's hand and pulled her out into the passage, closing the door behind us. We ran off into the yard and started filling buckets of water — only just in time. Ben's voice echoed out to us as he came downstairs.

'Mrs Mudge, tell that Robyn maid I want to see her. I've got another job for her . . . '

Annie and I huddled together, pumping up the water and hoping he wouldn't find us here, for he sounded angry. I wondered for a moment what had upset him, and then remembered Daniel Winters taking away the accounts book, and how Ben must feel about that. He was probably very disturbed, I thought, as we started carrying the buckets into the inn. Did he think the customs man would come again, and this time take him off to gaol?

My thoughts wandered into nicer places. Daniel Winters had said we might meet one afternoon by the Holy Well. I might go there tomorrow, just to see. Of course he might not have meant it, but I would definitely go. With the buckets slopping water as we walked, I felt a great longing to see him again. Yes, he was a customs man and I was a smuggler; but surely, somehow, we could remain friends?

Ben was in the doorway, his face puckered into a frown and his voice a hard growl. 'You, Robyn Lee — leave those old buckets and come here. I've got something for you to do.'

I hurried towards him, leaving my buckets outside the door. 'Yes, Master,

I'm here.' I stood in front of him and waited for my orders, my pulse a bit fast, my thoughts rushing off towards a mingled place of danger and excitement. What would he want me to do this time? No more crossing of the river, I hoped.

'Go into my little room and find the customs receipt for the tobacco which I bought legally last year. It's there somewhere on the desk; you'll just have to look. It's important for that customs man to see. I won't have him making me pay twice. Understand, maid?'

I nodded. This wasn't at all the job I had expected. Going through all that litter of paper on the desk would take hours and it would soon be time to go into the taproom. And I wouldn't be able to see once the light went. Reluctantly I said, 'Yes, I understand. But what does it look like, this receipt? Just a piece of crumpled paper, I suppose? And I'd better take a lamp, hadn't I?'

His face set and he said crossly, 'Just

stop making trouble and get on with it. You won't need a lamp yet; it's still light. And if you keep looking you'll soon find it. The receipt's just a piece of paper with the heading of the customs people on the top. So go on, now . . . '

'Yes, Master.' I heard disappointment in my voice as I turned, pushed past him in the doorway, and headed for the little room with the broken door. At least he didn't know I had been in there before. And, after all, smuggling wasn't always riding horses at night and being in danger, was it? Someone had to fill in the ordinary bits.

I was in the room, looking with dismay at the littered table, when he came in behind me and stood at my side. 'Important to find it, Robyn, maid, if I'm not going to be in trouble with customs. Do your best, won't you?' Now his voice was more friendly, and I turned to see him giving me a tight smile. Then I remembered Daniel Winters taking the accounts book, and realised I wanted to help Master Ben if

I could. I smiled back.

'All right, Master. I'll try and find it. But before you go . . . ' Something was making me turn and look up at the portrait of the young woman hanging over the desk. 'Who's that? Someone in your family?'

He shrugged, looked at the picture and slowly nodded. 'My old dad's sister, I think. Never saw her. He didn't talk about his family much, so I don't know why he's got that there.' He frowned. 'Why are you interested?'

I hurried to say, 'No reason, Master. But she was pretty, wasn't she? And well dressed. I mean, that lovely lace at her throat . . . ' That made me think of Annie and her longing to go to the lace school, but I knew this wasn't the moment to ask. Perhaps once I'd found the missing receipt Master Ben would be more approachable.

Ben made a sound like *hrmph*, and turned back to the door. 'Quick as you can,' he said sharply. 'I'll need you in the taproom before long. So get on with it and stop dreaming about pretty maids and nice clothes. This is much more important.'

'Yes,' I said, pushing aside my annoyance. 'I'll bring it to you soon as I find it, Master.'

He left the room and I began picking up the scraps of paper, trying to read what had been written on them some time ago. Most of the papers were damp, the writing running into blotched letters and hard to read. But I went on searching, and it came to me that Ben needed a helping hand to get his business into an orderly shape. Was it one more job I could do for the old Admiral?

9

I seemed to have been in that little
room for ages, and now I could see that
outside the sun was starting to set. I
was tired of trying to read all the
crumpled and blotched papers that
covered the table. They were mostly
invoices for deliveries of tea, snuff, and
lace, and something I couldn't quite
read that looked like muslin. But most
of them were concerned with tobacco,
and it made me wonder if most of
Ben's contraband goods were just that.
And then — at last! I found the invoice
I was looking for: a much-folded piece
of torn paper with big black writing
listing *2 tons tobacco*. It was finished at
the bottom of the paper, with *DELIV-
ERED* in block capitals, and then Ben's
signature, all untidy and scrabbling over
the page: *Signed, Ben Martin*. Thank
goodness I'd found it!

I went back into the inn, full of glee, and waved the dirty bit of paper in Ben's face when he came in from tending his boat on the foreshore. 'Here it is, Master! Do I get a reward for finding it? It was a really dirty job. That room needs a good clean-up . . . '

He grunted, took the paper and stuffed it into his pocket. Then he looked at me for a long moment before slowly allowing a big smile to spread over his face. 'You're a good maid, Robyn, and this paper will get that customs man off my back. All legal purchases, you see?' His smile turned into a grin, giving his face a softer and much nicer look. 'And so and you want a reward? Well, come here . . . '

Unexpectedly I was pulled towards him, his arms enclosing me. He kissed my cheek and then my lips. Then he stepped back and went into the taproom. 'This needs a drink to celebrate, I think. Come in here and join me, maid.'

I was uncertain what to do. Kisses I hadn't really wanted; a promise to let me take over more responsibility for the inn would have been better. But I was taken by surprise by the warmth of his arms and the softness of his lips, and found myself wondering if perhaps Ben Martin wasn't a nicer man than I had thought. Someone who might become my friend instead of my master . . .

But there was no more time to consider such muddled thoughts. A tankard was pushed into my hands and I was told to 'drink up, Robyn', which I did. Ben sat down on the window bench and gestured me to come sit beside him.

He said, 'We're a good couple, maid. You're a real help. And you can do much more in the next few days. I gotta go down to the customs people and show them this here bill so they'll know I bought this tobacco legally. And Mr Winthrop is paying another debt which they're on about, so I'll be quite safe now. No more snooping excise men coming round and making trouble! Another drink, eh?'

My head was swirling round a bit, so I said no very politely, and told him I must go and help Mrs Mudge in the kitchen. But before I went, I remembered about Annie and thought this was a good moment to see if Ben would allow her to go to the lace school in the afternoons.

'Lace school? What's that for, then? Annie's my apprentice; she does the pots. Who does them if she's not here?' He was frowning now, and I feared I'd chosen the wrong moment. But I tried to explain.

'Working as a pot girl won't get her anywhere, will it? But if she does all the work here in the mornings and evening, going to learn how to make lace in the afternoons will give her a chance of earning a better living as she grows up.' I didn't say anything about a better life. I didn't want to upset him.

I watched him think it over in his mind, and then he said, 'Oh well, I suppose she can. Who will pay the money?'

'I can give a bit, Master. And because she's such a willing girl, I wondered if you might . . . ' I stopped, smiled and put my hand on his arm. He looked down at it, and then at me, and that big smile spread across his face again.

'Part of your reward, is it then, maid? All right. You're twisting me round your little finger, aren't you . . . Well, I'll give her a few more pennies, and you must make all the arrangements. Only, don't forget those pots still need washing . . . '

Warmth ran through me. No, he wasn't such a bad man after all. I got up, leant forward and kissed his cheek. 'Thank you, Master. I'll tell Annie, and I know she'll work all the harder because of your kindness.' I turned and ran out of the taproom before he could say any more.

Annie and I worked hard that evening. I had managed to find a few minutes to tell her the good news, and now she was full of smiles as she washed the pots. Ben came into the taproom late in the evening. I guessed he'd been down in the village selling the fish he'd caught that morning. Now he was talking to some of his friends and I noticed them huddling quietly together at the back of the room, away from the noisy men around the counter. I made a point of walking towards them with a jug of ale and offering to refill their tankards. Ben looked up, then shook his head at his friends and sat back in his chair, saying nothing.

'More ale, Master? Or your friends?' I asked with a smile, but all I had was another shake of the head and a gesture to me to leave them alone. I did so, but I thought all the more.

When the evening came to an end and the everyday customers were drifting out of the door, homeward bound, Ben stood with his two friends, still talking. I watched them nod their heads once or twice, then Ben did the same. Finally they left, Ben coming back into the taproom by himself, looking as if he was thinking of other things than helping clear up the evening's mess. He disappeared, and I thought he went into his little private room with the broken door lock, but I wasn't sure. I had the feeling that he was busy planning something; and when Matt stumped in from wherever he'd been all evening and joined him in the private room, I knew I was right. Would it be another cargo run, perhaps?

After Annie had finished tidying up she went off to her bed in the kitchen, all smiles with her hopes of going to the lace school, and I climbed the old stairs to my little room that looked out over the river. The water was quietly flowing down to the estuary and it looked peaceful and lovely, with a half-moon shining down on it. But I knew it could be cruel as well as lovely like this, and I got into bed thinking there would probably be more adventures waiting for me with Ben.

But once in bed I couldn't sleep. I kept remembering Ben's kisses, and before sleep finally crept up on me he changed into Daniel Winters, and I knew it was him I would rather kiss. If I ever met him again. And then a last fading thought: how could he become my friend if I remained working with Ben as a smuggler?

*   *   *

He came in the morning. I had just woken and was getting up when I heard horses outside on the foreshore. I went to the window and there was a patrol of excise men — four of them — headed by Daniel Winters, who was dismounting and tying his horse to a post. I caught my breath, saw him head for the closed door and pulled on my shawl, ran my fingers through my hair, and grabbed my cap as I ran down the stairs.

He was knocking very loudly on the door and for a moment I paused before opening it. Why was he here? What could he want? Were we all being imprisoned and sent before the magistrate? But even with these awful thoughts raging around my mind I knew all I could do was open the door and find out what was happening. I drew the bolt and pulled the door back towards me.

Sunshine poured in but I hardly saw it. Daniel's face was set and his eyes had a cold look to them. He stepped in, removed his hat, and said politely, 'I have come to inspect the inn, Miss Lee. This is an official visit, so kindly allow me and my men to enter and go into every room. We will do no harm, and will leave once we are finished. No need for you to worry.'

I think he saw the fear on my face, for then he said more gently, and with a warmer expression on his face, 'It's all right, Robyn. Just let me look around.'

My head buzzed with thoughts. I was still afraid, but perhaps things weren't so bad. He had said nothing about a magistrate or taking us away, after all. I somehow managed a weak smile and said, 'Of course, Mr Winters. I don't think either Master Ben or Matthew is up yet, but come in and I will show you around.' I took a step away from him and waited. It struck me that if he wanted to look around the place by himself, that would give me a chance to warn Ben and Matthew. But even as I thought that, I heard footsteps above and a door banging, and guessed that both men were up and knew what was happening. I hoped one of them would come downstairs and take over from me. I was only a servant, and I shouldn't have to deal with all this.

Daniel was close to me, his hand on my arm, his eyes staring deep into mine. 'Take me around, Robyn. After all, you wanted to do that last time I was here. Well, now's your chance.' And he smiled! So perhaps he wasn't thinking of me as a wicked girl to be imprisoned or sent out of the country. I smiled back and felt myself lose all the tension that had filled me earlier.

'Of course,' I said. 'Please follow me, Mr Winters, and I'll take you into every room.'

He turned and spoke to the four men crowding in behind him. 'Stay outside,' he ordered. 'I'll call you if I need you. Go and look in the outhouses and that old cottage, and then wait for me.' Again he turned, and looked at me. 'Lead on, Robyn. I'm right behind you.'

I nodded, suddenly feeling much happier. His voice was as pleasant as it had been when we met at the Holy Well — deep and gentle. As if he was glad to be speaking to me . . .

'This way, then,' I said, leading him towards Ben's little room. 'Here is the master's office — and the door is open because last time you were here, you broke the lock.'

'I did,' he agreed, a step behind me. 'But only because you and Miss Annie refused to open it. I hope there won't be any more locked doors this time.'

He went into the room and stood

there, looking around. I saw him glance up at the portrait of the young woman on the wall above the bureau, give it a long look, and then slowly turn back to me. He was frowning slightly, as if something didn't make any sense. 'Who is this in the portrait?' he asked. 'But I don't suppose you know. Someone who lived here in the past, perhaps. But what I'm looking for is now, in the present. Like these drawers.' He pulled one out and tipped its contents onto the middle of the table.

I stood there, not sure what was going on, but watching and wishing Ben would come down.

10

Suddenly I remembered that Ben had given me the dirty receipt with orders to take it down to the customs house this morning. I felt it burning a hole in my skirt pocket and immediately pulled it out, handing it over to Daniel, who looked at it in frowning surprise.

'What's this?'

I said unsteadily, 'Master Ben told me to give it to you. I forgot . . . but here it is.'

He was looking at me very sternly. 'And why should Ben Martin want you to give it to me? Why can't he bring it himself?'

'I . . . don't know.' I heard my voice shake and wished I was somewhere else. The way he was looking at me was frightening, and of course I knew why — he was quite sure that I was a smuggler, just like Ben and Matt. I longed to tell him I wasn't, and take that hard look off his face, but it wouldn't be true, would it? I had helped Ben deliver his contraband goods, and so I was a smuggler just as he was.

I took a huge breath and tried to think how I could get out of this horrible muddle I was in, but no words came. Instead I heard Daniel ask impatiently, 'Where is Martin this morning? Is he in the house?'

I had no idea. If he was upstairs, then surely he had heard the noise of the men and their horses, and my conversation with Daniel Winters down here. So why hadn't he come down? I thought up excuses as well as I could, and finally said, 'Perhaps he's gone fishing. He probably went out early to catch the tide.'

Daniel raised one dark, well-shaped eyebrow. 'No, I don't think so. The tide was full when I left the customs house half an hour ago. He wouldn't have been able to get out of the harbour.' He looked at me with that stern look that scared me so much, and then said, 'I'll have to search the house. You can get back to your work. I don't need your help, thank you, Robyn.'

My heart fluttered. I wasn't going to let him out of my sight. I said quickly, 'No, I insist on showing you over the rooms. After all, I'm responsible for them, and you might not find your way,' which was a stupid thing to say.

He grinned slightly and said, 'All right, lead on then.'

I left the little room and took him along the passage, past the kitchen and the scullery, and finally up the winding staircase leading to the upper rooms. 'Don't trip, Mr Winters,' I called over my shoulder. 'The wood is old and has some rough knots in it.' He made no answer, but I saw him nod his head and then we were in the upstairs passage, with three or four rooms leading off it. I took him into the big room which I was planning to make into a welcome centre for visitors, and stood by the big window as he prowled around, knocking the wood paneling, looking up the wide chimney, and then coming to stand at my side.

I looked at him and managed a small smile. 'This will be such a lovely room when I've cleaned it up, lime-washed the dirty walls, and persuaded Ben to buy some new furniture for it. Big, comfy chairs, I thought, with small tables, pretty curtains and some sort of flooring that doesn't crunch under boots.' Suddenly I saw in my mind the lovely colourful carpet in Mr Winthrop's room. 'Rugs, perhaps,' I went on, 'or even a carpet . . . ' Then I stopped because of the way he was looking at me.

'You're full of dreams, Robyn Lee, aren't you?' he asked, his deep voice heavy with disbelief. 'And how do you imagine you'll get the Martin boys to make this room as you want it? They'll need a bit of money, you know. Fishing isn't going to bring in all that much, so where will it come from? Can you answer me that?'

I just stood there staring at him, knowing this was the one question I could never answer. Well, I could say gaily, 'Smuggling will bring it in, of course!' But that was impossible. So I said nothing, and knew he had me in the palm of his hand now.

'Well?' He was waiting for an answer.

I shook my head and looked down at the floor. 'I don't know, Mr Winters,' I said very quietly.

I heard him take in a deep breath as if he wanted to say something but decided not to do so. He left me at the window and went back to the door. 'All right, show me the other rooms. And any cupboards or storage places. Don't leave anything out.'

With my head whirring, I took him into all the upstairs rooms. They were shamefully dirty and full of rubbish, and I made a list of what I had to do up here. I must sort out the bits of old clothes, papers, odds and ends that didn't seem to have any use, and boxes which I hoped were empty and not showing signs of smuggling. The bedrooms were dreadful — blankets and pillows thrown all over the place, and the floors covered with empty tankards and lumps of mouldy tobacco. How could Ben and Matt live among this terrible rubbish? I wondered.

I didn't like to look at Daniel Winters's expression as we went into room after room and he searched in every likely place: up the chimney, and behind the chest which was supposed to hold linen and clothes, but just held rags now. On the landing there was a cupboard with a locked door and I looked at it, feeling really frightened. What might be in it? Daniel opened it with one heavy blow and all that we could see was cobwebs, green mould and heaps of dust and dirt. I took a look at his face and saw how tight his jaw was. This was proving to be a frustrating search, and I guessed he was getting angrier and angrier.

When we finally returned to the

staircase again he went down very slowly, arms upraised to feel the walls and ceiling above. I followed, wondering where Ben and Matt had hidden all their goods, if not here in the house. Had the men outside found barrels and boxes in the outhouses? And where on earth were the two brothers? They should be here, I thought, feeling myself getting angry as I realised they had left me alone to go through all this wretched searching with Daniel Winters. How dare they? I would have a lot to say when they finally came home. And what would the customs man do next? Having found no proof of smuggling, would he now leave us alone and try other places to search? And did that mean I would never see him again?

My mind was so busily engaged with all these muddling thoughts and fears that I came down the old staircase too fast, and suddenly felt my heel catch on one of those wooden knots I had warned Daniel about. Falling, falling . . . Arms reaching for the banisters and not finding them . . . A scream of fright filling the space around me and then, thank goodness, landing against something strong and warm. A sound reached me — 'Robyn, are you all right?' And I knew Daniel Winters had caught me in his arms.

It felt like all the breath had been knocked out of me, but at least I could just whisper, 'Yes, all right, thank you,' and hope that no injuries would suddenly fill me with pain. Slowly the shock of the fall left me, and gradually I began feeling happy to be held in his arms. It was like one of my dreams coming true. They were strong and warm, and I could even feel the beat of his heart through his coat as I lay there. I smiled to myself and wanted never to have to move away.

Then he was speaking, and I heard his voice very close to me saying, 'Are you sure, Robyn? No bones broken? No bumps anywhere?' His hands were moving over my arms, my shoulders, and then returning to where I had first felt them, around my body.

I closed my eyes. I was in heaven . . . until I remembered what was going on here at the inn, with Ben and Matt making use of me and turning me into a smuggler. At once I pulled away from Daniel, but he didn't let me go. Instead he drew me into a closer embrace and turned me to look at him.

There was a moment of amazement and surprise as our eyes met. I know mine were full of my raging emotions, which he must have understood, and in his I saw something warm and dark with wonder. It was as if we were seeing each other for the very first time, and exchanging all our thoughts and feelings.

His arms about me tightened, and I watched a smile lift his lips, happiness spreading over his face — until slowly it darkened again, and I knew where his thoughts had gone, with mine following them. I was a smuggler, he a customs officer.

We stayed, looking at each other,

until I felt him slowly — and it seemed reluctantly — releasing me. Then he spoke. 'I don't know what we can do about this, Robyn,' he said slowly, his voice deep and alive with his thoughts. 'But you must leave the inn at once. Go back to your home, lead a safer life . . . '

Something about those words ignited a new emotion within me: sharp refusal to give up what I was working for, what I wanted so badly — my new life here, renewing the Admiral, making a wonderful job of it. I pulled away from him and heard my voice grow quick and cool as I said, 'No! I can't do that, Daniel. You must just — leave me alone . . . '

As the impact of that awful, unthinking farewell hit me, I ran — down the passage, past the kitchen, out of the big door, and into the gleaming sunshine of the May morning . . . Running without thinking where I was going, and finding myself on the riverbank, where I gradually slowed down and finally came to a halt. I sank onto the mossy ground within a copse of shady trees, watching the water swirling past, hearing the river's soothing song, and wondering exactly what I was doing here. And what I was going to do next.

11

Slowly my thoughts quietened, and I felt more myself. But the knowledge that Daniel and I had exchanged feelings of great attraction — the word *love* hovered in my mind — was still there, never to leave. I smiled, wondering at the magic of our feelings. But — and this made the smile disappear — we were at odds with our different lives. If I stayed here at the inn, doing smuggling jobs for the Martin brothers, then I could have no more to do with Daniel. Indeed, I would become one of his suspects, and he would be duty-bound to try and catch me, along with Ben and Matt, in one of the deliveries of contraband which I knew they were continuing to plan.

Then I thought of Mr Winthrop, who seemed to be in control of Ben and Matt and their cargo-running. But because he was gentry and didn't go on these smuggling exploits, I knew the excise men would never bother him. Like the parson with his brandy, eyes would be shut to the small deliveries regularly made. Perhaps I might go and talk to him sometime and ask for his advice?

All these thoughts ran through my circling mind as I sat there watching the lazy river, enjoying the sun's warmth filtering through the trees, and waiting for an answer to my problem to come to me. For a while I had no idea what to do. Then I saw a pair of wild ducks swim up river, just beyond where I was sitting. The sun gleamed on the green and dark blue plumage and I realised this was a family, a father and mother followed by a little string of bobbing ducklings looking like a line of boats pushing their way through the small waves and rippling currents, in search of food. And at once I know what I must do.

Daniel's words suddenly rang through

my mind: '*You must leave the inn, go back to your home* . . . ' Yes, I thought gladly. I would take Annie down to the Ringmore lace school this afternoon, and then go home and see Ma and Father. Of course I wouldn't tell them of my problem, but I knew I needed to be with them again, to share in the love and strength they had always given me.

I got to my feet, ready to go back to the Admiral and wait for Ben to appear, to tell him of Daniel's search and then quickly, after the midday meal, go out with Annie and do all I had planned. With this running through my mind, a sort of quiet happiness returned, and I knew I would be doing the right thing. Forget the smuggling for a moment, even forget Daniel — as if I could! — and see what the day might bring instead.

When I got back to the Admiral, Annie was in the kitchen, helping Mrs Mudge with the vegetables. They looked up as I entered.

'Where've you been, then?' asked

Mrs Mudge with a frown.

I said easily, 'Oh, just out for a few moments. Something I had to look at . . . What can I do now to help?'

'Go and find the master. He's been looking for you this past half-hour. Out in the stables, I think.'

Annie looked up from the stone sink where she was scraping potatoes and gave me a look which I knew I must answer. I went to her side. 'Be ready to come with me this afternoon, Annie,' I told her very quietly, not wanting nosy Mrs Mudge to know everything. 'We'll go to the lace school. Master Ben said it's all right with him if you go, and he'll help with the money. Tidy yourself up, and we'll see what we can do.' I looked back over my shoulder. Mrs Mudge was turning from the fire and staring at me.

'Master'll be angry if you don't do as he says,' she said sharply. I nodded, then made my way out to the stables. But not before Annie had whispered, 'I got something to tell you. Not now

— later,' before returning to her scraping.

I found Ben in the stables. He was up in the tallat where the hay was stored, and came down the little wooden ladder as soon as I called his name. 'What did that customs chap want, then? And did you give him the receipt, like I said?' He stared at me without a smile, and there was a hard note in his voice.

I was angry. Why did he have to treat me like this when I was being so helpful? I said, 'Mr Winters inspected the house. I wonder you didn't hear him, as he went into all the rooms. And yes, I did give him the receipt.' I met his staring eyes and kept looking at him.

After a few seconds he nodded, moved away, and said, 'You did well, maid. Yes, I knew he was there, but I didn't want to see him. And he won't be back, not now that he's got the receipt showing that I paid for that cargo of tobacco. He'll know it's mine now and can do what I want with it, you see? That reminds me — low tide this evening, so I want you to take as many baskets as you can find and wait on the foreshore for what comes in.'

I frowned with disbelief. 'What comes in? On the tide, you mean? Washed up on the bank?' What on earth was he talking about?

'That's it. Small parcels thrown overboard the other night, see, and now coming home to me here.' He was grinning, smoothing the mare's nose before pulling down another handful of hay from the tallat above. 'So you go out there and pick 'em up, see? And bring them in to me. Then I'll sell 'em . . . make a bit of profit there, and no excise man to worry me anymore!' His grin grew even bigger. He stepped away from the mare, gave me a slap on the bottom and said cheerily, 'Good maid, you do that and I'll see 'bout that reward.' He marched off and I heard his boots clumping over the yard until the sound faded away and I supposed he had gone to the foreshore to see to his boat.

Slowly and very thoughtfully, I went back to the inn. The midday meal was nearly ready, and Annie and I were busy getting plates ready and helping Mrs Mudge with the pans and dishes. Ben didn't appear and I wondered if he was rowing down to the village and would eat something there. But I didn't bother much. Instead I thought hard about the afternoon ahead of Annie and me, and going to Ringmore to apply for her acceptance at the lace school. After that, I would go home. Like Daniel said, *go home* . . . I felt my smile grow as Mrs Mudge dolloped turnips on my plate, and was happier than I'd been for a long time.

The dishes were washed and put away, and Mrs Mudge settled herself in the chair by the banked up fire with a few last words to me: 'Don't be late coming back, Robyn. You're here to work, not going gallivanting about, you know.'

Annie and I left the inn. We both

smiled as we felt the sun on our bodies, and we pulled our hats lower down to keep the rays from burning our faces. I had some money in my pocket, and I knew Annie had a bit, too. I would have to remind Ben tomorrow that he had promised to help out with the charge for the lace school. It was thoughtless of him not to have handed it over today, but then I was beginning to understand that Master Ben only really did things for himself, and not other people.

'Come on, Annie,' I said, taking her hand. 'Let's go and look at the Holy Well as we go down the road. I haven't had any wishes coming true yet — perhaps I'd better make another one.' Of course, I was hoping that perhaps Daniel might be there. He'd said he'd meet me there one afternoon. Could it be now?

Annie's high, piping voice cut into my dreamy thoughts. 'You gotta give it time, Robyn. See, my wish is coming true quickly, but maybe yours will take longer.'

I came back to the present moment then, and knew she was right. Here she was, setting out to the lace school and hoping the mistress there would take her in. Well, half the wish was coming true, wasn't it?

We walked through Ringmore looking at the houses on both sides of the road, wondering where the lace school might be. I'd heard Ma talk about it, but didn't know any more than that many of the village girls went there to learn how to make lace. It would be a time-consuming job, I thought. Remembering that Annie had said she had started learning at the workhouse, I said, 'How do you make lace then, Annie?'

'On a pillow, with bobbins of thread. Takes a lot of time, and it's fiddly. You gotta have good eyes, but it's lovely . . . ' Her little face lit up, and I thought that this was a good thing, to allow her to do something that she so much enjoyed.

'Does the lace get sold?' I asked as I

looked at each house that we passed.

'Yes, grand ladies have it on their dresses or buy veils for when they get married. Some of the patterns are very old, and are only used by certain families.'

I stopped outside a house with a small garden. Just outside the door sat four children with small pillows on their laps, looking down at the bobbins they held and moving them about. 'Here we are,' I said. 'Come along, Annie — and make sure you smile when we speak to the mistress.'

It took a few moments for the mistress to come out and ask what we wanted. She was tall and very straight-backed. 'I am Miss Jackson and I run this school. Have you come to buy lace, or to ask to become a pupil?' Her voice was low and hard, and I saw Annie's smile fading already.

I made my own smile even bigger as I answered, 'Good day, Miss Jackson. I am Robyn Lee and this is Annie, who is an apprentice at the Martins' Admiral

Inn. Annie started learning lace work at the workhouse before she came here, and would like to take more lessons. She is allowed to attend every afternoon, and we have some money to pay your charges. I do hope you will take her in.'

Miss Jackson looked down at Annie, frowned, and picked up one hand and examined it. 'A small hand, but strong. What did you learn at the workhouse, child?'

Annie swallowed noisily, but found the necessary words. 'How to pin out a pattern, and then get the threads ready. And how to wash the finished lace before putting it to dry.' She stopped, and I saw the longing on her small face. Before Miss Jackson could say any more, she whispered, 'Please let me come, miss. I promise I'll work hard. Here are my pennies, and I'll give you some more when Master pays me.'

I saw a warmer expression spread over Miss Jackson's rather long, plain face, and heard a softer note in her voice as she said, 'This money isn't enough. But perhaps I might make an exception if you're a good worker. Come tomorrow afternoon and we'll start getting a pillow ready for you. Don't be late, for the hours pass very quickly once you're working and you need to make the most of the sunlight.'

I fished some more money out of my pocket and handed it to her. 'Perhaps this will help, Miss Jackson. And Master Ben Martin has promised to give some more.'

She took the pennies and looked at them very carefully before putting them in a purse attached to her leather belt. 'Very well. I'll take this on account. And Annie can only stay here as long as she works hard.' She looked down at Annie again. 'Remember that, child.'

'Yes, miss.' But Annie's shy whisper was stronger than I expected. She smiled up at the hard-faced woman, and then at me. 'Thank you for bringing me here, Robyn. I'll be here tomorrow after dinner. I'll run all the way and won't be late.'

'Yes, Annie, that's right,' I said. 'And now we'll go on to my ma's cottage and ask her for a drink of tea, shall we?' I held out my hand and she took it. Together — with a final bow of the head towards Miss Jackson, standing so tall by her door — we left the cottage and went down the road towards Apple Cottage, a few yards away.

As we went, Annie started singing softly, very high, her voice ringing through the little breeze that blew off the river. It was as if she was giving thanks for her wish coming true, and I listened with a warm feeling. If one wish could be granted, why not others? Would I be the next one to have a dream come true?

12

We reached Apple Cottage just as Ma was pushing the black kettle further over the range to make a pot of tea. She looked up with a big smile of welcome as we came through the open doorway.

'My word! And I was just thinking of you, Robyn, wondering when you'd come and see us — and here you be!' She looked at Annie. 'And who's this? Come and sit down, child. You look tired.'

That was Ma, of course, always thinking of other people and doing what she could do for them. I pushed Annie towards the chair Ma pulled from under the table and whispered, 'Tell her who you are and what you do. She'll be interested.'

I saw Annie flush as she sat down, neatly pulling her skirt around her legs and looking up at Ma standing by the fire, nursing the big brown teapot in her hands. 'I'm Annie and I work for Master Ben,' she said in a tiny voice. 'I wash the pots at the inn.'

Ma frowned. 'That's hard work for a little girl. How old are you, my love?'

Annie shook her head. 'I dunno, missus. I'm an apprentice from the workus. I think I'm about ten. Or eleven, p'raps. No one ever said.'

Ma put the teapot on the table, leaned down and took Annie's hands in hers. I saw her smile grow warm and wide. 'Well now, let's say it's your tenth birthday next week, and you'll come here to tea. I'll make a cake and we'll put a candle on it, and you can make a wish and blow it out.'

Annie's stiff little body grew easier in the big chair, and she smiled up into Ma's kind face. 'Oh, I'd like that, missus. Thank you. And I know what I'll wish for, and I know wishes come true, because of the lace school.'

Ma went back to the teapot still smiling at Annie, who now had nice red cheeks and a big smile, making her small face look bigger and happier. 'What's this about the lace school, then, maid? Not going there, are you? But you said you had to wash the pots at the inn . . . '

I said quickly, 'Master Ben is letting her go to the lace school in the afternoons, Ma. We've just been there to see Miss Jackson, and she's allowing Annie to start tomorrow. You see, Annie made lace in the workhouse and wants to go on doing it.'

I watched Ma's expression change. The kettle was singing now and she slowly made the big pot of tea, putting it on the hob to brew and then fetching mugs from the dresser at the far end of the room. 'Robyn,' she said over her shoulder, 'your Father's in the garden. Go and tell him to come in; he'll be ready for his drink of tea after working at those old vegetables on this hot day.'

I found him putting his spade and trowel away at the little shed at the end of the long, thin garden. 'Hallo, Father,'

I said, kissing his whiskery face and putting my arm through his. 'Tea's ready; Ma said come in now. And I've brought a friend with me — Annie works at the inn with me. She's a bit shy, so don't frighten her with your gruff voice, will you?'

'When did I frighten anybody, maid?' He was chuckling as we walked together down the path towards the kitchen door.

'Only when I deserved a fright,' I said, remembering stern words and hard looks when I was naughty as a child. Which was more often than I cared to think about.

He grinned at me. 'And now you're a good maid who works hard and has no problems.'

That made my smile fade a little. I couldn't possibly tell him about the smuggling, so I said hastily, 'Oh yes, everything's lovely. Master Ben is pleased with my work, and Annie and I are cleaning up the old Admiral. Soon it'll be like new.' We went into the kitchen after Father had kicked off his boots outside the door.

'In time for tea with our new little maid, Annie,' said Ma, putting a hand on Annie's shoulder and giving Father what I read as a warning glance.

Annie got up and looked at him with a timid expression. But Father was good with children and animals; he bent down to her height, held out his hand and said very quietly, and with a big smile, 'Delighted to meet you, Annie. Sit down and tell me how you like working at the Admiral.'

To my great surprise, Annie was smiling back at him, sitting down again and telling him all about the pots she had to wash after getting the buckets of water from the pump, sleeping in a warm but cramped kitchen, and being so lucky as to have me with her every day. Our eyes met once, but she was keeping quiet about the smuggling, for which I was thankful. And then I remembered that, this morning after Daniel Winters had left the inn, she had told me she had something to tell me. I was interested. What could Annie know that I didn't already? I told myself I would ask her as we walked back to the Admiral after our cup of tea.

We chatted happily for five or ten minutes, Father telling us how the mackerel shoals were smaller this year, and Ma saying that Mollie Black, the village gossip living next door, came in and helped her with the washing, which was greatly appreciated. Just as I was thinking we must get up and start our long walk back, she put down her empty mug and got up, saying, 'Talking about lace, I got something to show you, Annie. Stay here and I'll bring it down.'

When she came down again she had something in her hands that she carefully unfolded and put on the table in front of us. It was a soiled piece of thin, silky cloth, quite ordinary and not resembling any sort of clothing that I could make out, but it had an edging of wide, beautiful lace. Ma's hands smoothed it out and she looked up, meeting Father's suddenly narrowed eyes. 'Only the lace,' she said quietly, smiling at him. 'Just the lace, for Annie to see . . . '

We all looked at the piece of stained material and Annie, with a glance at Ma to see if she might touch it, and receiving a nod, ran her small fingers over the flowers and stems and leaves of the pattern making up the lace edging. 'It's lovely,' she said, her eyes wide. 'I saw lace like this at the workus — made by the ladies who looked after us there. Only not as fine as this. This is really — well — butiful.'

Such a long word for a small girl, but I could see from her expression that she was excited by what she was touching. 'Maybe I'll make something like this one day,' she said. She looked at me, then at Ma, who nodded and smiled, and finally at Father, who still wore that strange expression. But slowly his tight face eased.

He and Ma exchanged glances, and

then he said in a voice that was softer than I could remember, 'Mebbe you will, my love. If you're a good girl and work hard.'

A silence enclosed us then, sitting there in the warmth of the fire, and I felt a heart-warming fondness spreading around us, taking in Annie and making her one of our small family circle. I knew then that I had been right to bring her here, and that Ma was doing something special by showing us this soiled bit of cloth with its eye-catching lace edging. As I sat there thinking, she folded up the piece of material, looked at Father once more, and then took it upstairs. I heard a cupboard door being opened and then shut, and realised that for some reason that dirty bit of silk was important to Ma and Father. I wondered if I would ever know the reason for this secrecy.

But then my thoughts returned to the present moment, and I knew Annie and I must set out on our journey back to the Admiral. We mustn't be late, or

Master Ben would be cross and even perhaps stop Annie going to the lace school tomorrow. We said goodbye to Ma and Father, with shared hugs and kisses. Father watched us as we walked away, waving a last farewell before we turned the corner and left him behind.

Annie was quiet for a few moments, but then she turned to me and her smile was like a radiant shaft of sunlight. 'My birthday next week, Missus said, and she'll make a cake for me. I never thought anyone would do that. Oh Robyn, I'm so happy . . . ' She danced off down the street with me plodding along behind her.

What a lovely afternoon it had been, I thought. And for the moment my fears about more smuggling were left behind.

13

On the way back to the inn, I asked Annie the question which had been playing around in my mind since Daniel Winters's inspection of the house. Something she knew which I didn't. Well of course, she must tell me. I said, 'What did you mean this morning when you said you had something to tell me?'

I saw how she stopped dancing, waited for me to come to her side, and then fell into step with me, her face suddenly serious and excited. 'I found a hole,' she said, looking up at me.

'A hole? Where? And what was in it?' My curiosity rose swiftly. This must be another hiding place for Ben's contraband deliveries. Yet the excise men had searched inside the inn and outside in the stables and outhouses, and found nothing.

'I was looking in one of the rooms at the top, up in the attic, cos I heard you and Mr Winters come down from there and I wanted to see if it wouldn't make a nice bedroom for me, for that old kitchen's so smelly. On the wall was a lovely picture of the harbour, and I wanted to see it better, so I touched it — and it fell down. Oh, I was scared that Master Ben would blame me. But just as I was picking it up again I saw a sort of knob on the wall, and I touched that too — and the wall opened.'

I stopped, put my arm on her shoulder and turned her to face me. 'The wall opened? Annie, what are you talking about? Walls don't open, for goodness sake.'

Her mouth curved upwards. 'This one did, Robyn. I'll take you up there and show you when we get back.'

We started walking again, and now I was keen to reach the Admiral and see this unlikely hole she had found. I thought hard. Perhaps it was a rat hole — we'd heard them in the roof — or just a bit of lime-wash falling off to reveal a small space between building stones. I asked, 'What was in this hole?'

Annie took my hand as if to soothe me. 'It was a little room,' she said slowly at last, 'with a chair in it, an old box, and lots of parcels all crowded on top of each other. It looked like someone had been in it, though — a half-empty pot was on the floor among piles of rubbish, and everything smelt of smoke.'

Things were starting to make sense. Ben and Matt were smugglers, I knew that. And yet when the customs patrol searched this morning, nothing was found. So what if most of the goods were hidden in Annie's hole? I couldn't wait to get back and see for myself just what was going on in the Admiral's attic.

We managed to slip upstairs without Mrs Mudge seeing us and telling us to come and help with the evening meal. When we got to the passage at the foot of the stairs where I had fallen into

Daniel's arms, I stopped for a moment and felt a great smile spread over my face. I began wondering when I would see him again. Perhaps tomorrow at the Holy Well?

Annie looked back over her shoulder halfway up the stairs. 'Come on — it's up here. But why are you looking so happy, Robyn?'

I couldn't tell her, of course. Her question made me think once more about the awful difficulties between Daniel and me. Smuggling. If I was a suspect he was trying to catch, would he really ever come to the Holy Well again? By the time I reached the top of the stairs I knew my smile was long gone, and I had to make myself think of something else. Like the wall that opened in the attic, just a few steps down the corridor.

We went in and stood there, looking around. The afternoon sun had gone down slightly, so the room was shadowy with no light. But I could see that it might make a nice little bedroom for

Annie, which would be far more comfortable than that lumpy old truckle bed in the corner of the kitchen. Another favour I would have to beg from Master Ben. Which brought me back to the question at the back of my mind — where was he? And where had he been all the time Daniel searched the house? I felt myself getting angry now; it was too bad of him to leave me to face the excise men like that. I would tell him so when he appeared again.

In the middle of all that thinking, Annie had gone to the wall where the picture of the harbour hung, removed it, and then touched the small knob that stuck out. And yes, the wall opened . . .

I gasped. There was filth everywhere. The little room was crowded with parcels and small barrels against the far wall, a pot with ale still in it, and a strong tobacco smell. Suddenly I knew where Master Ben had been this morning when he had heard the arrival of the customs patrol — in this little room. I turned, looking for some way of closing the wall. Nothing. And anyway, even if he had managed to close the wall when he was inside the room, the space of the missing picture would still tell anyone that something odd was going on here. So it must have been Matt who shut Ben in here and then swiftly left the house by the back way, not seen by the excise men outside. And when Daniel and I were up here, searching, Ben had been just a few feet away, listening to us, and smiling as he knew he was safe — another reason to be angry with him, for he hadn't cared that I had been with Daniel, and could have been blamed if any contraband was found.

I took Annie's hand and pulled her out of the little room. 'Come on,' I said. 'I'm going to find Master Ben and tell him what I think of him. Let's go down and see if he's come back.' We closed the hole, replaced the picture, and I drew her towards the stairs, shutting the door behind us.

But Annie was reminding me of things I had conveniently forgotten. 'Wait a minute, Robyn,' she said, her voice suddenly nervous. 'You mustn't make Master angry, because if you do then he won't give me the money he promised, and might not let me go to the lace school tomorrow. Oh, please, don't make him change his mind . . . '

I heard tears not far away, and had the sense to stop raging about Ben's unfair treatment of me, and think about Annie. No, I mustn't make him angry. She was right. So I calmed down a bit, and by the time we were downstairs again I was ready to help in the kitchen and then spend the evening in the pot room. When Ben did come back to the inn, I would wait for a quiet moment and then very carefully say that we'd found the hole in the wall, and could he explain, please? I expected him to say it was a safe hiding place.

And then another thought — would it be foolish to tell Ben I knew about the attic? He wouldn't want me to know his secrets, even if I did some jobs for him. I remembered that he had said he had another job for me — to take baskets and collect whatever the tide left on the foreshore as it went out. I guessed that what it was I picked up would be taken up to the attic room and hidden in the useful little hole, which Daniel would never know anything about. Oh, how clever Master Ben and his brother Matt were.

Annie and I worked on during the early evening, and then Ben came stumping into the taproom and nodded his head at me. 'Come outside,' he said. I followed him out, thinking that I had no wish to go and pick up the things the tide might sweep in this evening. I was tired, and he must give me some time in which to rest.

We came to a halt by the ruined cottage door at the back of the inn and he turned and looked at me, his eyes narrow and his face stern. 'So what did that customs man say this morning? I heard you talking to him.'

That did it. My anger got the better of me. I pursed my lips and knotted my hands stiffly in front of me. 'So if you heard us, why didn't you come down and talk to him yourself? Why leave me to do all the business with him?'

He looked amazed that I should speak so roughly. His brows came down, heavy and unattractive, and he took hold of my shoulder and shook it. 'Don't you speak to me like that, you maid, you. You'm my servant and you gotta keep quiet, and not go on so.'

I pushed away his hand and took a step backwards. I said carefully, 'I know I work for you, Master Ben, but I'm just the taproom girl. I don't have to do dealings with customs men for you and you better understand that.' We stared at each other, and then I remembered the end of the morning search, with me falling into Daniel's arms, and all my rage disappeared. I managed a small smile. 'Sorry, Master, but I gotta say what I feel. And this morning was very difficult for me.' Oh yes, how difficult.

157

I watched his face ease a bit. The dark eyes opened more and then he nodded, and again his hand touched my shoulder. But this time it was gentle, more like a caress. 'You're right, Robyn. I should have been there with him, but it wasn't safe, so I let you do it. And you were clever, maid. You gave him the receipt and then got rid of him. And they never found anything, all those men on their horses sniffing round the stables and outhouses.' Again he nodded at me, and his smile was wide.

I didn't know what to say next. I still held it against him that he had left me to face up to Daniel, but I didn't want him to know that I knew where he'd been hiding. Something told me to keep quiet about the wall with the hole and all the goods up there. I didn't know why, but instead I said, 'Well, perhaps you'll let me off the picking up of whatever the tide brings in tonight. I need a good rest. Perhaps tomorrow . . . ?'

He frowned again and shook his head. 'Course not! Gotta be done tonight with that tide washing in. Look, maid, I'll help you. Just get the baskets together and when the taproom closes we'll go together. I'll carry 'em on the old horse, and then you can run back and get to bed. Will that do?'

I supposed it would have to do. 'All right,' I said grudgingly, 'so long as you do the carrying. I'll go and find the baskets now and put them ready, shall I?'

His smile was full of satisfaction, and he nodded. 'Off you goes, then. I got see to my boat.' He pulled me towards him, put his arms around me and kissed my cheek, saying, 'You're my girl, aren't you, Robyn?' He left me standing at the old ruined door as he swung around the corner of the cottage, disappearing onto the foreshore.

I was left feeling surprised. Ben, kissing me again? Making out I was his girl? But I wasn't. I didn't want to be. I wanted Daniel Winters to be close to me, saying those words . . . But as I returned to the inn to search out all the baskets, I knew I was dreaming something that was most unlikely to happen.

I was still smuggling with Ben and Matt, so how could Daniel think anything nice about me at all? The thought took the gentle expression off my face, and made me frown because I couldn't see a sensible way ahead. I needed someone to help me. But who?

14

It was dark and misty when Ben and I left the inn behind us, he leading Lady and me carrying as many baskets as I could handle, down to the riverside. The waters were quiet now, flowing gently along with none of the roar and surge of the other night when Lady and I made our way back from the far bank.

Ben tied the mare to a post halfway up the beach and joined me at the water's edge. Yes, as he'd said, there were many small little parcels and barrels washing up on the sandy foreshore — not very big, and carefully wrapped in oiled canvas, easy enough to pick out of the water and stow in one of the baskets.

Beside me Ben reached far out for the ones I couldn't handle and between us we soon filled the baskets. He was grinning as he said, 'Expect you're wondering where these come from, maid. Well, I'll tell you. They was thrown overboard from one of my mate's boats in the dark last night and now they've washed in by the tide for me to take in. Customs duty paid — well, that bit of paper you give to the excise man said so — and now I can sell 'em again, see?'

His grin grew bigger and I turned his words over in my mind. So that was what Daniel was looking for. I had helped Ben in this tricky bit of smuggling, although Ben would have honest money when he sold all the goods a second time.

When the last package and barrel were safely landed I stepped away from the water and stretched my arms and shoulders. It had been a hard job pulling them all in and I felt really tired. I thought of my bed and was glad when Ben started carrying the baskets back to Lady and securing them to the sides of her saddle.

He looked back at me and grinned.

'Home you go, then, maid. You done a good job — deserve a rest, you do. And I haven't forgot that reward I talked about the other day. Mebbe soon I'll have something to give you. Like that, wouldn't you, eh?'

I said carefully, 'Depends on what it is, Master.' Without really thinking, while watching him with the baskets, I added, 'as long as it isn't anything smuggled . . .'

He looked up at that, and his smile was gone. 'And what's wrong with that, then?' he asked in a hard tone. 'Not telling me you've gone to the other side, have you?' Suddenly his voice sharpened and his eyes narrowed until, through the misty darkness, I could hardly see them. 'Cos if you do, you'll have trouble with me, maid. An' remember, folks don't make trouble with Ben Martin if they can help it. I'm warning you, Robyn . . .'

He stared and I stepped away, for I thought he looked as if he might just throw more than hard words at me. I remembered Annie finding the pistol upstairs, and knew then that I must stay on the right side of the Martin brothers if I valued my safety. I said quietly, 'Sorry, Master; of course I didn't mean anything. Shall I carry those two baskets you can't get onto her back?'

I knew it was cowardly of me, but at the end of this long day the last thing I needed was threats and bad feelings. *Bed*, I thought hungrily. *Please let me get there.*

We still had to carry all the baskets upstairs and put them in the passage where the attic door was. I knew Ben would hide them in the little hole, but I said nothing and was thankful when the last basket stood there and he nodded his head at me. 'Off you goes, then. You looks as if you're going to sleep standing there . . . ' He grinned and I knew I was forgiven. For the time being.

'Thank you, Master.' I turned and made for the stairs, but his voice followed me.

'You're my girl, so call me Ben, see?'

What could I say? Weakly I smiled over my shoulder, took the first step down and muttered, 'Thank you, Ben.' Then I ran to my bedchamber as fast as I could.

* * *

Next morning I found the passage empty, which meant that Ben had stored all his goods in the hole in the attic. Going down to the kitchen, I found Mrs Mudge very grumpy because he'd been up early, demanding something to eat and saying he'd got to be away quick. 'Off down the river, he was,' she said crossly, 'and me still frying his bacon.'

I was glad he wasn't here. Now I would have the chance to clean the little room where he kept his books, and no one would bother me. I was collecting the cleaning box when Mrs Mudge said, 'Here, Master left this for you. Said you'd know what it was for.'

She handed me a few pennies and my heart beat a little faster as I realised these were to help pay for Annie's afternoon schooling down in the village. So Master Ben wasn't quite as mean and hard as I had been thinking.

I told Annie about the money and saw her face shining with joy. 'I'll take it this afternoon,' she whispered, and I noticed how her smile was easier and bigger. 'Miss Jackson'll be happy to have this. Oh, how kind Master Ben is,' she whispered before going off to the sink to start washing the huge pile of dirty pots waiting there.

I thought her words over and realised that Ben was a complicated man, neither bad nor good. Perhaps I had misjudged him? But one thing I was sure of — he was very different from Daniel. And that made me decide that I would go with Annie this afternoon, as far as the Holy Well — for who knew whether Daniel might be there?

I tidied and scrubbed the little room where Master Ben kept the accounts until late in the morning, humming Annie's little song about the sprig of thyme to myself, when the door opened and Mr Winthrop came in. I sat back on my heels and moved the bucket of water out of his way. 'Good morning, sir.'

He looked down at me and I saw amusement in his deep eyes. 'On your knees, Robyn? Well, time to get up, I think. Sit down here and tell me about all these papers.'

I was glad to do so, and sat opposite him at the table. He shifted some of the papers and raised spectacles to his eyes to read the faint, washed-out words. 'These are mostly illegal invoices,' he said at last, crumpling a handful of them in his large, powerful hands. 'But one was for a legal purchase. The customs office has it now, and Winters is surprised that Ben actually paid for those goods.' He looked at me very keenly. 'He said you gave it him. Do you know anything about it?'

I remembered what Ben had told me

last night. 'As he paid tax for the tobacco, he had it brought back here and now he's going to sell it again. Only this time he'll keep the money.' I paused. His face was tight. 'Isn't that all right, Mr Winthrop? Or will he be chased by the excise men again?'

He leaned back in his chair and stretched his legs beneath the table. Slowly, he said, 'Nothing that Ben Martin — or Matthew — do is ever strictly legal. So far, because of my friendship with their late father, I've managed to square things with customs. But now I feel I've done enough. And customs, too, are anxious to catch both brothers and bring them to book for all the smuggling activities they've carried out in past years. And are still doing. You see, I believe a big delivery is in the offing.'

I held my breath. That meant more contraband coming ashore, more risks, and more work that Ben would insist I help with. I thought of the money he had given towards Annie's schooling, and knew that I must do whatever Ben asked. I knew he was quite capable of withdrawing the money if he thought fit. So I had to continue being a smuggler . . .

Mr Winthrop was looking at me with a thoughtful expression on his face. 'Robyn,' he said at last, 'isn't it time that you stopped helping Ben and Matt with their smuggling? Do you really want to have the excise men after you, as well as them?'

I sucked in a long breath and thought hard. I couldn't explain what hold Ben had on Annie and me, for Mr Winthrop might well offer to pay for Annie himself, and I knew that wouldn't be fair. Also, if she and I stopped working at the inn, where would she go? Back to the workhouse, I supposed, and that was something I could never allow. So no, I had to keep working here, and look after the little maid.

'Well?' he said, and I realised I hadn't answered his question. I decided it would be best to pretend that I had no fears about being a smuggler, so I said brightly, 'No, Mr Winthrop; I'm happy here at the inn and Ben is being kind to Annie and me. I'll carry on as I'm doing, but thank you for suggesting I should stop. I don't do much to help, after all, and I'm sure no one knows that I'm part of Ben's little company.' I gave him my best smile and got to my feet. 'And now, if you'll excuse me, I must get back to my scrubbing.'

I was on my knees again as he rose, went to the door, and then looked back. I saw him staring at the portrait of the young woman hanging over the bureau. He narrowed his eyes and then said, 'Same colour of hair as yours, Robyn. Beautiful.'

I looked up, too. And something made me say, 'Not nearly the same as mine, Mr Winthrop. Mine is really red; hers was a lovely sort of sand colour.'

He nodded and smiled down at me. 'But still, there's a likeness, you know.' He paused and then, almost as if he disliked what he was saying, said slowly,

'I have done the last bit of smuggling that I intend to do, giving false information to the customs officer so that Ben and Matt can land this big cargo. I would like to think you will keep well clear of anything to do with it, Robyn.'

We looked at each other and I knew my eyes were wide. He had told me a very dangerous bit of information, and I started wishing I didn't know anything about it. But I couldn't pretend I didn't know, could I? For the truth was that I was bound to smuggling, in spite of my new longing to escape. I said unsteadily, 'Thank you for telling me, Mr Winthrop,' and left it at that.

He nodded, his face very sober. Then he smiled faintly, turned, and said over his shoulder as he left the room, 'Watch how you go, Robyn.'

I heard his footsteps echoing down the passage until the big door shut behind him, and then his horse slowly walked out of the yard and I was left, still on my knees, scrubbing brush in hand, thinking hard about all he had said.

15

Annie and I walked away from the inn once the dinner dishes were dealt with, and I saw the excited expression on her face. It made me think that my decision to keep in with Ben was the right one, even though by now, and after all Mr Winthrop had said, I had new thoughts about smuggling.

The afternoon was warm and the river looked like a silver thread floating majestically along towards the sea. It dawned on me that rather than being only a pathway for smuggled goods dealt with by greedy, rough men, it was also a natural and helpful thoroughfare. Good things came from the river, as well as cargos of contraband; what about fish, and boats, and lovely shells, and wild birds? And all those strange things washed up by the wide and mysterious ocean.

I was happy to listen to Annie chattering on about making lace and how one day she would make me a collar — a tucker, she called it — to put on my best dress and wear to the next May Fair on the green. 'I'll make it in a pattern that everyone knows, and then when they see you wearing it, Robyn, they'll know which family you belong to. Yes, really, they will.'

Suddenly she looked so serious that I was quite touched by her loving thoughts. I knew then that I must keep looking after her. Whatever happened, I wouldn't let Ben keep her away from learning this new, wonderful craft that clearly meant so much to her.

We reached the Holy Well and I stopped there. I saw the impatience on her face, so I said, 'I'll just stay here for a few minutes, Annie. You mustn't be late for Miss Jackson, so hurry along. You've got the money, haven't you? And make sure you come back to the inn in time to help with the pots this evening.'

She smiled at me, saying, 'All right,

Robyn. Why, perhaps your wish will come true, now you're here again.' She trotted off down the lane, pausing at the corner to look back and wave.

Her words echoed in my head as I sat down on the grass beside the well, and I smiled to myself rather sadly. Just because her dreams were about to come true didn't mean mine were, too. In fact, the more I thought about smuggling and Daniel Winters, the more I realised that my dreams were just a load of nonsense, never to have any reality.

I sat there, idly playing with a piece of grass, listening to the bees buzzing around a nearby daisy, and wondering what to do next. Perhaps I would go down and have tea with Ma — but something told me to wait here. And in a little while I was so glad I had stayed . . .

I heard horse's hooves on the flinty lane just above the well, and then spotted the flash of remembered blue through the hedge. I scrambled to my feet, hardly believing what I instinctively knew to be the amazing truth — Daniel was here. I could have shouted with joy, for he had remembered saying he would meet me here one afternoon, and now he had come.

A strong arm parted the hedge and he came through it, leading his horse. Seeing me, he stopped and I waited, breathless, for the smile I so longed to see. Yes, it was there — slow, but warm and full of something that made my blood sing.

'Robyn', he said slowly, holding out his hand. I took it in mine and we looked at each other without saying anything, but I sensed that in our hearts we were saying it all. I wanted this moment to go on and on — for nothing else to happen; just to stay here in this lovely dream, with Daniel holding my hand and looking into my eyes. But I knew that life doesn't stop; it goes on, and we have to do what we can with it.

So, very slowly, I took my hand from his and said quietly, my voice a little shaky, 'I'm so glad you've come, Daniel. I want to talk to you — if you can spare the time.'

He turned, tied the horse to a branch and then looked back at me. 'Of course I can, Robyn. That's why I'm here — for I want to talk to *you* — and it's important that you listen.'

Another moment of silence, and I felt the world start to shake around me. He knew I was one of Ben's smuggling party; was he about to say that he must arrest me?

I sank down on the grass where I had been sitting before and said in a quivery voice, 'I'll listen, Daniel. So tell me what you have to say.'

He joined me on the turf and half-turned so that he was looking directly at me. My eyes met his. I knew mine were wide and nervous while his, the sea-green of a quiet sea, were steady and even somehow reassuring. 'Why do you look so afraid, Robyn? Words can't hurt you, and I hope mine will help you to sort out the tangle you have got yourself into. You know what I mean, don't you?' He reached across the small space dividing us and took my hand. He looked down at it, amusement on his lean, handsome face. 'Such a small hand for your big, brave spirit. But it's red and sore — have you been cleaning more rooms at the inn, Robyn?'

I gulped. Smuggling? No, cleaning! Was this what he wanted to talk about? I said, 'Yes, Daniel, of course I have. I won't rest until every room has been tidied and scoured and made to look beautiful.' I heard my voice strengthen and I was able then to give him a proper smile. 'You'll see a difference if you come again . . . ' That brought me back to thoughts of smuggling and more searches by the patrolling excise men, but something gave me a new feeling of courage and I added, 'And that's what I want to talk to you about. Ben and Matt Martin and their smuggling.'

He was silent, still looking at me, then he said, 'And your part in those

177

activities, Robyn.'

I bowed my head. He knew. Of course he did. So what would he do about it? Quickly I tried to make foolish excuses. 'I don't do much,' I said very fast, not looking at him now. 'Just helping sometimes — little things, like carrying a basket, or — or something like that . . . '

His free hand came beneath my chin, making me look up and face him. 'But I fear that your *something like that* is enough to brand you as a proper smuggler, Robyn. You see, I have information about all the runs that the Martin brothers make, and already you are named as being involved in them.'

'Oh,' I said, and felt foolish as well as afraid.

Then he dropped his hand and looked at me sternly. 'I don't think you understand the risks you are taking, Robyn. I know you feel you must be loyal to the Martins, but to become a smuggler is quite wrong. For one thing, you're a girl, which is very shocking, and also vulnerable to the dangers you run. Smuggling is full of hazards — difficult cliff paths and rough tracks — and even violence when things go wrong. And another thing: have you thought about what people might say about you? What your parents and family would think if they discover just what you're doing? Truly, Robyn, you should leave here and go back to the village. I want you to be safe, you see.'

I sat there with thoughts racing through my mind. I understood that there was truth in what he said, but surely nothing was as bad as the picture he painted? I was only doing very small errands for Ben . . . At last I heaved in a big breath and said, 'But Daniel, it's important that I stay here at the Admiral. It's my job, and also I have to look after Annie. Ben is paying her a little more so that she can go to the lace school every afternoon. I wouldn't want that to stop.'

I watched him think about it. Then

he frowned, saying, 'Why is Annie so important to you? Is she part of your family? Why should you have to look after her?'

'Because she's an orphan, and an apprentice to Ben. And if he gets rid of her then she'll have nowhere to go except back to the workhouse, and I couldn't let that happen, could I?'

The frown eased into the wonderful smile which I had loved right from the first moment of meeting him. 'No, Robyn, you couldn't. Not you with your warm heart and sense of caring for people.' His voice was warmer, softer, and he looked at me so kindly that I felt even more churned up inside. What a terrible muddle all this was. What was I to do now?

I knew that because I had to remain working for Ben, I must still agree to run his errands. And yet Daniel had told me exactly what might happen, which was frightening. I gathered my fading strength and asked him very unsteadily, 'Suppose you found me doing it — smuggling, I mean. What would you do, Daniel?'

The kindly expression grew tight. 'I would have to do my duty and arrest you, Robyn. You would be locked up while all the paperwork was prepared, and then sent to Exeter, where after a day or so in prison, you would appear before the magistrate.'

My eyes locked with his. My voice was almost inaudible. 'And . . . and then?'

Daniel hesitated. Then he took my hand again and said gently, but with a note of sadness, 'Either years in gaol, or even transportation to a foreign land.'

I swallowed loudly. Images swirled around my mind: what Ma would do, what Annie would do, how the village would think badly of me; and my hopes for a new, clean and attractive Admiral Inn were completely wiped away. And yet . . .

There seemed only one thing to do. Panic had me in its grip, and I hardly knew what I was doing as I stood up, looked at his questioning face, and said in a shaking voice, 'I'm sorry, but I have to go. I'll be careful, I promise I will, Daniel. But I can't stay here any longer.' Then I ran.

16

What a relief to reach the Admiral and hide myself upstairs in my bedroom. I needed time to calm down, to think over all that Daniel had said, and somehow work out how I could keep my job here and yet avoid all the dangers he had described. Perhaps, I told myself after a long, quiet time of sitting looking out of the window and listening to the song of the river and feeling the sun on my face, Ben wouldn't want me to do any more errands. But inside I knew that was unlikely. What had he said about me being his girl? About giving me a reward? That didn't sound as if he was letting me off the hook.

After a little while of thinking and planning and not really reaching any useful decision, I decided to do a bit more cleaning. Anything would be better than sitting here doing nothing and worrying. So I went and fetched the household box of dusters, cloths and brushes, and went up to the big room which I was planning to turn into a beautiful, clean and attractive parlour for all the visitors who would come once they knew about the Admiral's new look.

I swept, dusted, wiped clean the bleary windows, and began imagining the curtains I would make to celebrate the shining panes. I thought of Mr Winthrop's elegant room and decided these would be long, reaching the ground, made out of thick material to keep out the draughts, and decorated with flowers. How nice that would be. And perhaps a new carpet to bring out the colours I had decided on . . .

'Robyn — where are you, maid?' Ben's rough voice sounded up the stairs and at once I was brought back into the difficult present moment.

I shook my duster clean in the fireplace and put the brushes back in the household box. 'Up in the parlour, Master,' I called once my heart had stopped racing. I went and stood by the door. What did he want? Was it one more errand? And then all Daniel's warnings came like gunshots into my churning mind. How could I get out of this terrible muddle?

Ben came thumping up the wooden stairs. He stopped just inside the doorway and stared at me. His face was thunderous, and at once I felt afraid. What had happened? Were the customs men after us?

'My brother!' he bellowed, fists curled and expression full of hate. 'Gone to sea, he has. Got a berth on a brig sailing for the cod fishing in the Grand Banks, and left me with all that stuff to deliver. Not a word about going. Why couldn't he have warned me? We could have got rid of it by now. But off he goes, and I'm left here to do it all! My brother — huh!' He spat on the floor.

I stood motionless, watching as he

slowly walked towards me. As he moved so, his face altered, the terrible expression very slowly changing to one of what looked like relief. He came to my side, stared at me, and then began to smile. 'But I got you, Robyn, haven't I? Well now, maid, you gonna have to help a bit more than you expect. There's this last big run we need to do before the end of the week when the lugger comes into the harbour again, with the moon waning. So tomorrow, see . . . '

He nodded, the smile grew, and he was almost chuckling when I broke in, shrill and alarmed, with, 'What lugger? What do you mean? And surely you have friends who can help? Not me! I mean, I'm only a girl, not strong enough to . . . ' I stopped.

The frown was back in place. He gripped my arm, pulled me towards one of the old chairs lining the walls and almost pushed me onto it. He stood looking down at me, and his voice was determined. 'You gotta help me, Robyn.

You're my girl. And now Matt's gone I need you, so tomorrow you can take the gig with Lady . . . '

'But I can't drive a gig! I don't know how!'

He shrugged and said quickly, 'You're good at learning; you'll soon know how. I'll tell you what you need to know, and Lady's slow and trustworthy. You won't have to go far; only down into the village, taking Mrs Clifton-Jones her bale of silk, see.'

I was thankful to be sitting down, I felt so weak. So yet again I had to do as he ordered and risk being caught in the delivery of contraband. Thoughts rushed around in my head and I said unevenly, 'But if someone stops me they'll find the silk, and then I'll be arrested. I won't do it!'

Ben leaned over me. His eyes were narrow and full of steely purpose. 'You'll do as I say, maid. Otherwise those extra pennies I give Annie won't come no more. And she might even be sent back to the workhouse as being useless. Think about it, Robyn. You'll drive the gig. 'Why look,' is all anyone will say, 'the maid from the Admiral, out for a bit of a spree, eh?' You'll take that silk and you'll be back here afore anyone knows it. So make up your mind, see?'

I sat there in silence for what seemed like several minutes, while he still stood at my side. I heard his heavy breathing and understood that I was caught in a trap from which I saw no escape. Finally, because it seemed like fate had me in its grip, I said weakly, 'All right, Ben. I'll do as you say.'

The next morning Ben ordered me out into the yard, where Lady was standing in the shafts of a very shabby gig which had once obviously been smart but now was covered in peeling and fading paint. 'Up you get,' he said, and then sat beside me. 'Now, here's how you hold the reins. Like this . . . ' Then he told Lady to 'walk on' and she slowly moved around the yard, with me afraid that she might suddenly rear or start galloping out into the countryside. I wondered, if that happened, if I could safely jump to the ground, and if Ben would come and rescue me. But slowly, with Lady behaving so well and my confidence growing, I began to understand just how to take control of her.

Beside me, Ben chuckled. 'Told you you'd soon learn, didn't I, maid? Good. Well, this afternoon you can take the stuff down to Mrs Clifton-Jones. Won't take you more than an hour and then you'll be safely back again. After dinner I'll give you the stuff. Now, leave me to untack Lady and you get on with your cleaning.'

I went back into the inn with my head full of new thoughts. Yes I felt safe with the gig, and I only had to drive down the hill and into the village — the Clifton-Jones' mansion wasn't far away — and then I would return to the inn and perhaps no one would notice me. And such a small errand — surely Daniel wouldn't even get to know about it. My confidence grew even stronger and I returned to the dusting, sweeping and scrubbing with more feelings of hope as I remembered his kindly words of warning, and that beautiful smile ... Perhaps things would all turn out for the best, after all.

Ben called me into his little room after dinner. He had a parcel on the table and was unwrapping it. There was an oiled canvas, then a great piece of soft Hessian. I thought, *This must be quite valuable, judging from the care that's been taken of it.* And then — a small bale of pale blue silk, glimmering there in the sunlight that came streaming through the window.

'Oh,' I breathed. 'It's lovely.'

★ ★ ★

Ben nodded and grinned. 'Mrs Clifton-Jones only wants the best. She'll pay a good price for this, so make sure you bring it straight back, see?'

My thoughts began to darken. I hadn't realised that I would be carrying money on the return journey. But then I told myself that it was only a very small errand, perhaps the last he would ask me to do, and so I was hopefully on the way to finishing with smuggling, as Daniel had asked me to do. I fingered the silk, wondering whether I would ever have a dress made of such delicate, rich material as this. 'I'll wrap it up again, shall I?' I asked Ben, but he shook his head.

'Only one way of carrying this. Off with your apron and dress, and wrap it round your middle. So, if you get stopped, no one'll know you got it there, see? Clever, eh?' He laughed.

I was shocked. 'I can't do that!' I said sharply. 'How'll I get it off when I arrive at the house? I can't just undress . . . '

'You'll go to the back door, tell the maid that you've a message for the missus — something about the dress you're making for her — and then she'll take you up to her private room, her boudoir, where you can strip off and give her the silk. Easy.' Suddenly he frowned. 'And don't make no fuss about it, maid.'

I stared at him, thoughts circling. I realised now that if no one knew I was delivering contraband goods, then I was safe. And no one would ask me to undress, so what was I fussing about, as Ben so roughly put it? I said slowly, 'All right then. So go and put Lady in the trap while I wrap it round me.'

I watched him leave the room, then went and made sure the door was safely closed before I took off my apron and then my dress, carefully unrolled the material, and began wrapping it around my middle. With my dress tight around my waist again I could hardly feel the silk, so soft and thin it was; and I couldn't help a spark of delight filling me, for this was the first time I had worn silk — and of course the last. But it was a brief moment of pleasure, and when I went out into the yard I climbed into the trap feeling more sure of myself than ever.

Ben waved me off. 'Hurry back,' he

ordered, 'and keep the money safe. I've got things to do, people to see.' His face fell into a scowl and he added, 'That demmed ol' brother of mine, going off like that and leaving me to do it all alone. Well, I gotta find some mates to help out, so I won't be back 'til later. Put the money in my room, see? And shut the door.'

Obediently I said, 'Yes, Ben,' and then told Lady to walk on, which she did, slowly and without trying to gallop off. We drove down the hill, along the lane and into the village without any problems, and by the time we reached the first cottage I was quite enjoying myself.

★ ★ ★

The Clifton-Jones' mansion was an imposing building set back from the road through the village, and I worried as I drove the gig around the back of the house to the stables whether anybody would gossip about me arriving here. All the village, I knew, liked to chat about Mr and Mrs Clifton-Jones and their visitors coming to stay, the wonderful dinners they gave, and the summer garden parties in their beautiful grounds. Would anyone include me in the gossip? I was breathing fast when I left the gig in the care of the groom and went to the back door.

A maid dressed in a smart black dress with a white apron opened it and looked at me curiously. 'Yes?' she asked.

I took a big breath and smiled politely. 'I have a message for Mrs Clifton-Jones,' I said. 'It's from her dressmaker. Will you ask if she'll see me, please?'

The girl stepped back. 'Come in. You can wait in the kitchen while I go and see madam.'

In a few minutes I was led up a huge staircase lined with big portraits all the way up, and into a room that overlooked the river. Mrs Clifton-Jones looked me up and down. 'A message, you said?'

I gulped. 'From Ben Martin, madam. I've, er, brought what you wanted . . . '

She smiled, eyes shining greedily. 'Ah, yes. So where is it?'

Another big breath. 'Under my dress, madam. Shall I, er . . . ?'

The smile grew. 'Please do. I will draw the curtains.' She rose and went to the big window. They were heavy, I noticed, and terribly expensive — all that lovely brocade stuff. I quickly unwrapped the silk and placed it on the little table beside her chair.

She sat down again and fingered the silk, opening the bale and letting the material flow down to the floor from her lap. She glanced up at me. 'Such a beautiful gown it will make.' Again a smile, greedier than ever. 'Tell Martin I'm pleased with it.' The smile faded. 'And I suppose you'll carry back the payment?'

'Yes, please, madam.' I was eager to leave now that the material was safely delivered. I thought I was safe; there was only the money to carry, and that could be tucked into my skirt pocket where no one could see it. I took the small purse she handed me, made a curtsey and said, 'Thank you, madam, and good day,' and hurried away from her boudoir, down the stairs, and into the kitchen where the maid, busy setting tea cups of lovely thin china onto a tray, stared at me. And then out into the yard. Lady was waiting, and we drove off quickly out of the long entrance to the house, into the lane, up the hill, and nearly home. Oh, the relief. I thought it was all over and I was safe. No one had seen me or would know what I had done.

And then, coming over the brow of the hill, was a figure I knew: Daniel Winters on his grey mare. I panicked — he mustn't see me, not with this purse of free-trading money so heavy in my pocket. All the old worries returned, darker than ever. I must hide somewhere — thank goodness a farm entrance was in sight. I drove Lady into it and managed to hide the gig behind a huge stick pile in the empty yard. No one there to make a fuss. I sat there, my breath coming very fast, listening to the hoof beats passing the entrance and then fading as Daniel rode on down the lane.

Only as I judged it safe to come out of the farmyard again, did it dawn on me that my mind was in a chaotic state. Hiding from Daniel? When all I really wanted was to be with him. I realised bitterly then that my life was getting even more muddled as the days passed. Somehow I must get better control of it.

17

It was late in the evening when Ben appeared in the taproom together with a little knot of men, all of them as shabby and rough as he was. They sat at a table in the far corner, away from the counter, and I watched them talking and gesturing to one another until eventually Ben got up and his friends slowly disappeared through the big doorway.

He came up to me and looked at me with a frown, his eyes searching mine. 'Did it, did you, maid? And got the money? In the room, is it — safe?'

I wiped a spilled mess of ale on the counter and said quietly, 'Yes, Ben. It's there, and I don't think anyone saw me.' I said nothing about Daniel passing in the lane and me hiding from him. Better to keep things hidden as far as my feelings were concerned, I thought.

Ben's tight expression eased and he gave me a bit of a smile as he walked away towards his little private room, leaving me and Annie to clear up all the mess of the busy, hard-drinking evening. Annie looked at me as she piled her tray with dirty pots. 'What was he talking about, Robyn? What did you have to do?'

I thought quickly. No point in worrying her. So I said casually, 'Oh, just a little errand. Didn't take long, but I learned how to drive Lady in the gig. It was quite exciting.' As she nodded, smiled and disappeared with her heavy tray, I thought to myself unhappily how my life was becoming more and more involved in muddles and deceit, which wasn't how I wanted to live. I must change it somehow.

In the morning Ben pulled me into his little room as I was on the way upstairs to start some more cleaning. 'I gotta talk to you, Robyn. Come in here.' He banged the door shut and we sat opposite each other at the table, which was still piled with papers. He found the purse with Mrs Clifton-Jones's money and stowed it in his pocket with a greedy smile. 'I told you 'bout the lugger coming in, didn't I?' Narrowed eyes stared at me and I felt myself becoming even more anxious, for I feared he was about to involve me in yet another smuggling trip.

I thought back for a moment and then said warily, 'Yes, but I didn't know what you were talking about.'

He sat back in his chair and pulled a face, showing his bad teeth. 'Well, 'tis time you did know, so I'll tell you. The lugger's the big ship carrying the next load of contraband, and it's due to anchor just outside Ness Beach beyond the harbour next week, when the moon's at its lowest. It'll be dark — a good time to unload. And even with Matt skiving off, I've still got friends who'll help me get on with the job. And you, maid — you've gotta help, too.' Now he began to smile, and I feared what would come next, for Ben smiling meant something bad, as I had learned already.

I said sharply, 'I'm not going to help unload, if that's what you mean. That's heavy work for men, not maids.'

'No, not unloading. Something more clever. Something you'll like to do.' His smile grew and my heart started racing.

'And what's that?' I asked fearfully.

'Going down to customs and talking to that Winters man. Telling him where the unloading will take place.'

'What? But . . . ' I was confused.

'No, not what you think, maid. No, you tell him the wrong place, so that when the lugger anchors we'll be somewhere else, safe away from any nosy excise men. Henry Winthrop has already suggested to him that there's a little smuggling bay by the big rocks at the far end of the beach, so he'll jump at the idea of catching us. Clever, eh?'

I was shocked into silence. Go to Daniel and tell him a downright lie? I couldn't do it. If he found out, he would never want to see me again. I felt anger start to burn inside me and said very firmly, 'I'm not going.' In my head I imagined Daniel listening to my tale and giving me that stern look. I added strongly, 'Even if I did go, he'd never believe me. And anyway, how should I possibly know where unloading is going to happen? No, Ben, you can't make me do that.'

His expression darkened and he bunched a fist on the table, hitting a pile of papers and causing them to fall to the floor. 'You'll do as you're told, maid, and that's all there is to it.'

We looked at each other for a stretching moment, and then, very slowly, his face slid into a sly smile. 'He'll believe you cos he's got an eye for you, and you know it, don't you? Surprising what a pretty maid can do to a man who feels soft about her . . . So all you got to do is put on the charm and tell him you just happened to hear that the lugger will be anchoring up by the Parson and Clark, in that little cove where we've offloaded many a time afore. Only this time — ' Now he was chuckling. ' — he and his mates'll waste their time at the far end of the beach, and we'll be somewhere else!'

At first all I could think was, how did he know about my feelings? He was cleverer than I thought. But what could I do? My anxiety grew, for I knew what would happen if I didn't take the message to Daniel. Darkness crept around my thoughts. Then again in my mind I saw Annie's little face, so much brighter now that she had started learning lace-making, even becoming more sure of herself. I knew that Ben had me in a hateful and inescapable trap.

I stared at him and guessed that my face showed all my feelings. Impulsively, I said, 'Give me time to think about it, Ben. I can't just decide like that.'

I didn't really expect him to say yes, but I saw his smile become thoughtful, and then he nodded, saying quietly,

'You're a good maid, so I'll give you 'til this afternoon. You can go down to the village as it gets dark, cos that's when Winters is there, back from his daytime patrols. All right, go off and do your cleaning. But remember — ' He leaned across the table so that I sat back, suddenly afraid. ' — you gotta go, and that's all there is to say.'

I got to my feet in a hurry, ran out of the room, picked up my cleaning tools and climbed the stairs. Anything to get away from Ben and his frightening demands. As I settled into the scrubbing routine in one of the filthy guest rooms, I wondered ridiculously if anything might happen this afternoon to stop me from going down and lying to Daniel. And as I worked away I sadly realised that nothing could happen. I would have to go. It was a terrible thought, and I kept imagining Daniel's expression when I started to tell him the tale.

It was a relief when Annie called me down for dinner. She sat beside me at the table, chattering away about what she was learning. 'Miss Jackson is pleased with me, Robyn. She says I've got quick fingers and a clear mind. And she lets us sit outside in the sun with our pillows and talk, as long as we get on with the work. I'm making friends with some girls in the village — just think, friends! I never had any before!'

I saw her eyes shining and I knew then that I had to take the message to Daniel. It was with muddled thoughts running around my head that I helped wash the dishes, and wasn't aware that the knock on the door had brought a young boy from the village until Mrs Mudge came to the scullery and said, 'This young lad's come up from the village with a message for you, Robyn, so you better come and see him.'

At once my worries increased. A message — and from whom? I ran to the kitchen door where a lad I recognised as Barnaby, living just up the road from Ma and Father, stood waiting. 'What is it, Barnaby?' I asked, pulling him into the yard where Mrs Mudge and Ben wouldn't overhear us.

He grinned and fidgeted around on his big feet. 'Your Ma,' he said. 'She told me to come and find you and tell you you gotta go home. She needs to see you urgent, she said.'

I nodded. Words failed me. Was Ma ill? Was this another terrible worry that I must deal with? I said unsteadily, 'Go and tell her I'll be down sometime this afternoon.' I found a halfpenny in my pocket and gave it to him. 'Thank you, Barnaby. Did my Ma seem quite well?'

He pocketed the coin with a big grin and said lightly, 'Think so. But she said it was urgent, so I run half the way up here.'

'I'm very grateful. You're a good lad. Now run back again and tell her I've got the message. And I'll be with her as soon as I can.'

I watched him swing around and march out of the yard, smiling back over his shoulder as he did so. And then, slowly, he ran down the lane, leaving me full of uneasiness and indecision. Could Ma be ill? I must go and see her, of course I must — but what about Ben's orders to go and see Daniel Winters, too? I paced around the sunlit yard for a good five minutes, trying to plan out my next move.

18

Annie came out of the inn, about to go down to her lace class, which made me decide to go with her and then branch off to see Ma and Father. I decided I would stay with them until it was dark and then make my way to the customs house. I knew I still hadn't decided whether or not to tell Daniel Ben's made-up story about the next offloading. I felt very uneasy about it. I didn't want to tell any lies, but Ben had said I must, and I knew what the result would be if I refused. And seeing Annie with her smile and more confident manner, my feelings about it all were even more disturbed.

I walked along the lane with her, listening to her chatter about the lace and the pattern she was following, and how the other girls asked for her help because they weren't as quick as she was, and it became more and more obvious that I had to do as Ben said. I wondered, as we walked, if I could somehow just *suggest* the wrong off-loading place to Daniel without making it seem really so. Could I say I had heard Ben talking to his friends and they had mentioned the Parson and Clark rocks off Smuggler's Cove? Of course, I would also say I had no idea if that was the actual place the lugger would anchor.

But I knew that was yet another lie, for I did know — the lugger would anchor round the Ness headland in the little beach which had a tunnel specially dug out of the cliffs for smuggling. I would probably be left to look after the horses when the men went down the tunnel to collect the contraband. Then I would be part of the small procession of horses and carts that made their way through the moonless dark up the lane and across the river again, and then on, up to the wild moorland and the long road to Exeter.

I shook my head to try and clear it of the awful pictures I imagined, and Annie said anxiously, 'What's the matter, Robyn? You're not listening to what I was saying, are you?'

'Of course I am!' I raised my voice cheerfully and she went on telling me little bits about her afternoons in the school.

We were close to the Holy Well, and as we approached she said, 'I expect your wish will come true soon, Robyn. Think how fast mine worked!'

I was about to say I didn't think it was working at all well, when we heard horse's hooves coming up the lane, and suddenly I had a wonderful thought that this might be Daniel off on his patrol. Oh to see him now, when I was feeling so upset and not sure what to do; for a smile from Daniel would surely heal all my troubles. I stopped quite still and waited, and then yes — he appeared, trotting up the lane.

But no smile. He stopped, looked down at me, and frowned. Then he said, his voice chilly, 'Where are you off to, Robyn Lee? An afternoon to yourself, perhaps? No errands today?' He dismounted and led his horse off the track, while I stood quite still and felt the warmth which I had hoped for leave me. Instead I was growing angry and uncomfortable.

Annie stifled a laugh and said, 'I'll go on, Robyn. I mustn't be late,' and ran off down the lane, while Daniel tied his reins to a sapling tree and then turned and looked at me. His eyes were keen and I felt they were suspicious. For, of course, he thought of me just as a smuggling maid, always doing something which was illegal.

That brought words rushing into my mouth. 'Daniel, please believe me, I'm not doing anything wrong. I'm on my way to visit my ma and father, who want to see me.' I heard the pleading in my voice, felt my hands twisting together, and then saw how slowly, he began to smile. Not the rich, warm smile that I longed for, but a gentle, understanding expression which calmed me and made me start to feel everything might still be all right.

He looked at me for a few seconds and I waited for what he was going to say, for clearly he was thinking hard. And finally he said gently, and so quietly that I knew he was expressing his inner thoughts, 'I'm glad to hear, Robyn, that you're just having an afternoon to yourself and going to visit your family.'

I didn't answer. No words came into my head, and all I could do was bask in the warmth that slowly spread across his face. His voice was warm. 'Why don't we sit down by the well, like we did last week? I'm on my way to see Mr Winthrop, but he can wait. Give me your hand . . . '

I did so, and he helped me sit on the fresh green turf by the well head. I heard the water rippling as it bubbled up through the ground, and felt a strong yearning that my wish might come true. We looked into each other's eyes and he stroked my hand as he said, 'So you're off to see your family. And I was afraid you were out on yet another of Ben Martin's errands. Well, I'm glad I was wrong. Have you been thinking about what I said yesterday? That you must give up working with him, and leave the inn to find a safer situation?'

This wasn't what I expected to hear. He was so determined. Would I ever safely escape his suspicions? Once again, my problems ran around my mind. I slid my hand out of his and said, 'It's not so easy as you think, Daniel. There are reasons why I must stay at the inn, you see.'

'Tell me.' He sat back and looked serious again, and I knew I must choose my words with great care.

'It's Annie. Ben will send her back to the workhouse unless I carry on working for him, and I can't let that happen, can I?'

'Annie . . . I see. But her life isn't important enough for you to risk your own, surely? If Martin ill-treats her, or doesn't keep to the terms of her apprenticeship, the justice will deal with him.'

He was looking at me very intently and I felt my cheeks start to flush. I thought he would have understood. I thought for a moment, then said sharply, 'I can't just leave her be. She's young, and shy, and . . . ' I stopped. I hoped he would have agreed with me, but no, he was plainly stepping back into his customs officer way of thinking, and I saw how his face grew stern and thoughtful again.

At once I, too, slid back into my own thoughts. All right, so he didn't understand my caring for Annie. He wasn't as warm and kind as I had hoped. So I wouldn't allow myself to be turned aside from the order Ben had given me.

We sat there among the grasses and daisies, and I began to plan how to give him Ben's message. I played for time, saying innocently, 'Daniel, why are you going to see Mr Winthrop?'

His expression grew tighter. 'He brought me some of Martin's accounts to check a week ago — seems he acts as his accountant — and I'm now returning them.' He paused. 'And also to ask him about a rumour he'd heard and passed on to me that a new contraband cargo is due to come into the harbour soon at Smuggler's Cove, the little bay at the far end of the beach. If there's any truth in it I must get my men armed and ready.'

I took a deep breath, for here was a fine chance to tell him that not only Mr Winthrop but I, too, had heard the same tale. Eagerly, I said, 'the Smuggler's Cove by the big rocks, and the Parson and the Clark?'

He looked at me suspiciously. 'How do you know?'

'I've heard men at the inn talking about it.' Yes, Ben had done so. I wasn't having to tell a lie, and I had passed on the message safely. I felt so glad that it was all working well, and I would have asked him to sit beside me for a while longer, but suddenly he was on his feet, looking down at me. No smile, just the expression of a man going off to do his duty.

'I can't stay. Winthrop will wonder where I am.' He strode away and untied his horse. Then, looking back over his shoulder, he mounted and said coolly, 'Enjoy your visit to your family, Robyn, and keep out of trouble if you can.'

He returned to the lane and rode off, leaving me forgotten and alone, with tears not far away. I stayed where I was for a few minutes longer and then bravely forbade myself to think any more about Daniel Winters. I rose and washed my hands and face in the well, whispering once again my wish, and then set off down the lane, eager to see Ma and Father and learn why they wanted to see me so urgently.

*   *   *

Ma was making pastry at the table when I went into the cottage and at once she put down the rolling pin, wiped her floury hands and came to me, hugging me, kissing my cheek and whispering, 'Oh, I'm so thankful to see you, maid. I hoped you would come today. You got my message, then.'

I pulled out a stool from under the table and sat down, smiling at her, wondering at the expression of anxiety that lined her face. 'I'll get your father in,' she said, scurrying out into the garden.

I sat there relishing the warmth and fragrance of my home and realising how much I missed everything about it. For the moment I even forgot Ben and his free-trading and the stern look on Daniel's face as he left me a while ago. But then Father stood in the doorway, kicking off his boots, and Ma was at the table again; only now she put aside the pastry-making and looked at me as if the world was going to fall apart.

'Whatever is it?' I asked, suddenly afraid of yet another new trouble.

19

Father came in, sat down heavily in the cane chair at one side of the fire, and nodded to Ma to sit down opposite him. They both looked at me and their faces told me how worried they were.

I sucked in a big breath, knowing I needed some new strength to face whatever this might be about. 'Tell me what's the matter,' I said unevenly.

Ma's eyes moved from Father's leathery face to mine, and slowly she said, 'Well, maid, we've heard some tales about you. Seems the village is full of gossip . . . '

'That's nothing new,' I said heatedly. I thought a bit and then added, 'I expect having Mollie Black as a neighbor hasn't helped things, cos she's known as a terrible story-teller.'

Ma nodded and her mouth worked as if uncertain what to say next. Then she said, 'That's true, but the trouble is that she's talking about you, maid. And it's going all round the village.'

My stomach lurched. I knew that village gossip always ran round the houses, but never before had it been about me. It was a horrid feeling. What were they saying? I cleared my throat and said hoarsely, 'So what's it all about? Tell me, for goodness sake, Ma. Tell me . . . ' But instead of telling me she wiped her eyes, and I realised with a shock that all this was bad enough to make her cry. I moved fast, went to her side, knelt down and put my arms around her. 'Tell me,' I said urgently. 'It can't be so bad. What've I done? Please, Ma, tell me.' She bowed her head and I felt her heart beating fast through her shabby dress.

It was Father who told me. His voice was steady, but I heard all the distress in it as he said roughly, 'They do say as you're in with the smuggling band, maid. And that you go helping with the deliveries of contraband. Not only that, but the customs officer is after you, and that he'll catch you any day now. And then . . . ' He stopped, and I saw all that he wasn't saying in his eyes. Being arrested by the preventive men. The shame of being hauled before the magistrate; the guilty sentence, and then into gaol at Exeter waiting for, at least, transportation. And the rest of my life spent somewhere in the world where I didn't want to be.

I must make excuses. But there weren't really any, were there? Or tell them I wouldn't be doing any more of it — but then, what about Ben taking revenge on little Annie? I went back to my stool and stared into the kettle on the fire. It was quietly humming; that kind and gentle sound which made this cottage such a warm and a loving home. It made me understand how badly I had behaved and how I was hurting my mother and father; and I knew then that all I could do was to tell them how sorry I was.

I sucked in a big breath and said

slowly, 'Yes, I've been doing small errands for Ben Martin, and that means I've been helping with his smuggling. I thought it was just a bit of an adventure at first, but now he's told me I must keep helping. So it's true what people are saying, and I wish with all my heart that I'd never done it.'

I couldn't meet Father's keen eyes, so I looked down at the rough matting on the floor and wished bitterly that I could undo the past few weeks. Ma dried her eyes and looked at me in a strange way, and I wondered what she expected me to do. Eager to make amends, I said unsteadily, 'I'm sorry to have hurt you so badly. I'll have to tell Ben I won't do any more errands, won't I?' And then I thought about his orders that I should tell Daniel about the next offloading, and I felt all the old worries crash heavily on my shoulders again. How could I tell Ben I refused to help him any more?

Ma remembered what I had told her. Slowly she said, 'But what about little

221

Annie? Will Ben Martin refuse to pay her school fees if you don't do any more for him?'

'Yes,' I said heavily. 'He's warned me about that. And even said he would send her back to the workhouse.'

Ma sat up straighter. She looked at Father for a moment, and then back at me. 'We'll take the maid in here if he wants to do such a bad thing. Send her back? No, he won't!'

I smiled a bit wearily. So that was one good thing — Annie's future was safe. But what about me? 'I think she'd love to come here, Ma. And she's learned to be very useful, too. You wouldn't regret taking her in. But I can't come back . . . '

'You want to keep on working at the Admiral?' asked Father, and I nodded, so strong in my mind was the wish to keep on cleaning the old place up. Even if Ben still continued smuggling, I wanted to carry on with my dream of improving the inn and making it a paying concern. I wondered then that if

I told Ben to stop smuggling, on the understanding that I would need his help to get the rooms repaired and furnished and decorated, would he agree? After all, the Admiral was his property, left him by the old captain. Between us I was sure we could make it a profitable inn once again.

These new thoughts were positive. I said in a brighter voice, 'I shall keep on with the plan of improving the inn. Ben Martin will just have to help me, and give up his free-trading. He said I was his girl, so he must be prepared to work with me, surely?'

Ma suddenly choked. She looked at me with horror. 'You can't be that ruffian's girl! He's no good! Just a common smuggler — you don't want no more to do with him, maid. You're worth more than what he can offer!'

I sat up very straight, surprised. I said, 'But I'm just a villager, too, like him. How can I be worth any more?'

Neither of them answered, but I watched them exchange looks and saw the doubt on Father's face, and the growing determination in Ma's eyes and set mouth. Then she surprised me even more by getting up and hobbling to the stairs, saying, 'I'm going to fetch something you should have had years ago, maid. And I'm going to tell you the truth . . . '

We sat silently, Father and I, until she came down again, and then she put a small bundle she was holding onto the table in front of me. 'You've seen this once,' she said, 'when I showed it to you and Annie admired the lace collar. Well, now you have to keep it, because it's all part of your life before you came here to us, you see, maid.'

I caught my breath. What was she saying? 'My life? Before . . . ?'

Ma sat down again and nodded. She suddenly looked much stronger, more able to deal with all the troubles surrounding us. 'You weren't born our daughter, Robyn,' she said slowly, looking now at Father and giving him a smile that spoke of enduring love. 'We couldn't have no children, so when Father found this little scrap washed up by the storm, he picked you up and brought you home here, to me. And I cared for you as our baby. Loved you, like we do now and always will. And cos of that red hair, we called you Robyn. There now, what d'you think of that?' Her smile was full of love, easy and warm, her faded eyes shining.

I had to pause for my breath to return. All this was well nigh impossible to believe. Then I said, 'Picked me up? What, out of the sea?'

Father chuckled. 'Aye,' he said. 'There was a big storm that November and the wreckers brought the ship onto the rocks, where it foundered. Many souls drowned, and your mam must have been among them. But I couldn't watch a babe drown, could I? So I grabbed you, dripping wet, and wrapped you under my coat. Cos no one would have understood — all they was thinking about was looting all they could from the ship, and valuables from the drowning people.'

'Wreckers?' I asked slowly. I'd heard rumours of such folk, who tied lights to their donkeys and tethered them on the cliffs to lure a big ship onto the rocks below and then to salvage everything they could see in the wreckage that was cast upon the shore. And people were left to drown; yes, I'd heard such stories and never hoped to believe them. But now . . .

I looked across at Ma, who was watching me with a faint smile that told me she and Father expected something of me in return for all they had given me during my short life. And now I knew what it was.

I said heavily, 'So it was smuggling that brought me here. It was the reason why the wreckers wanted the ship on the rocks: to gather the goods and sell them. And I've been smuggling, too, without knowing what a terrible thing it was. So now I have to stop it.'

Silence wrapped us together for a little while. I knew all our thoughts were churning away. Seeing that terrible image of the wrecked ship crashing against deadly rocks . . . People trying to save themselves; people drowning . . . Could my mother have been among them?

As the pictures slowly faded, Ma pushed the little carefully wrapped package across the table and said quietly, 'Open it, maid — cos it was all you wore that night: just a scrap of material, soaking wet and not properly covering you. But it's yours and you must keep it safe, now that you know the truth.'

My hands shook as I opened it. Of course I knew what it was; Ma had shown it to me before — a strip of silk with a big patch of lace at one end. Not part of baby clothes, but something of my mother's — a petticoat, perhaps, torn and wrapped around her baby in a last loving gesture before the waves and the wreckers did their worst?

I folded the square of ravaged silk and pushed it carefully beneath my bodice, next to my warm breast. It was safe there — all I had to remind me of where I had come from, and who I was.

I went to Ma and kissed her, then turned to Father and did the same. They were watching me and when I quietly said, 'I have to go now — I have something important to do,' they just nodded and smiled. I knew they trusted and loved me, as they always had done. Nothing had changed.

But everything was changing. I left Apple Cottage with warmth surging through me, and determined thoughts focused on what I knew I must do next.

20

I knew where I was going: just one place to show me where I came from. Where my mother wrapped me in that piece of silk before she fell into the water. I walked very fast down to the harbour and then along the road leading to the headland, and there were the big black rocks. I stopped, suddenly finding it hard to breathe . . .

It all looked so calm and lovely this late afternoon. The tide was slowly coming in, small ripples of scalloped lace washing over the golden sands. Fishing boats were moored and others were out there in the ocean, just beyond the sand bar, with nets and lines catching mackerel and pilchards; lobster and crab pots were ready to pull in, to keep the families alive and earning their livings. I stood there on the sunlit beach and let my thoughts wander.

November, Father had said. A huge storm. Lights on the donkeys tethered on the cliffs. The passenger ship, full-sailed, caught in the current, and the fierce waves powering around the slanting deck. Passengers staring around them, praying that the ship wouldn't capsize. I shut my eyes, the picture was so awful, as a final seventh wave pushed the ship onto those huge black rocks. The sound of crashing timbers, of cries for help; hands reaching out to hold other hands; raised voices praying for survival. And then the end, and the smugglers snatching at whatever the waves brought to the shore.

I forced my eyes to open. I had to face it all. Mother had perhaps fallen from the deck, her arms around me. The baby in the water. Father standing there, wanting to help everyone — and then snatching me up, hiding me in his jacket, running home through the wind and the gale to Ma in warm little Apple Cottage. And me, the baby, taken in and loved for the remainder of my life.

When I had come to terms with the sad story, I turned back to the village and began walking towards the customs house. I knew now that smugglers had been the cause of my mother's death, and now I must do my best to stop Ben and his free-trading. Somehow I must put an end to the smuggling in the village. It was wicked, even though no wreckers were about these days. Yes, I must stop the smuggling.

The sun was slowly sinking in the western sky, the colours changing from brilliance to softer shadowy, yet more fiery, shades. It would soon be dark and I could go and find Daniel Winters, as Ben had ordered me. Only this time I would tell him the truth — that the lugger, in a few days' time, would anchor in the Ness cove, and not the Smugglers' Bay at the end of the beach. I would explain why I was there: to try and help him catch the smuggling band, and stop all the free-trading that the village enjoyed. It was the least I could do, in memory of that terrible storm and the capsized ship — and my mother's death. I quickened my steps. I hoped Daniel would be there, and that he would believe all that I had to tell him.

As I walked through the village I thought about Annie, hoping that she had returned to the inn and was safe there. I would have to tell her that Ma and Father would like to take her into their home, and that she mustn't worry about Ben sending her back to the workhouse. I wondered how the lace-making was getting on, and knew that, back at the Admiral this evening, I would show her once again the lace on my piece of silk. She was interested in it before, so now, with growing knowledge, she might know a little bit more about the pattern.

The streets were shadowy now, and I stepped out quickly towards the customs house, thinking at the same time that tomorrow I must go and see Mr Winthrop. I would tell him about the storm and my mother's death. And I would also tell him that I had decided the least I could do was to somehow stop the smuggling that Ben was doing. I knew he had said he was the supervisor, which I suppose meant that he didn't actually help with the smuggling — so perhaps he would agree with me and try and put an end to the free-trading in the village. But if he didn't, I would have to do it on my own.

My thoughts ran back to the hidey-hole at the inn, and to the pistol that Annie had found in one of the bedrooms, and I felt a small shadow of fear creep through me as I neared the customs house. But then as I saw it, brick-built and strong, a new feeling came: one of pleasure at seeing Daniel again, and a great hope that he would believe me, and help me in my mission to stop Ben and his wicked smuggling.

I was working out in my mind what I would say; how I would describe all that had happened and what Ben was, in reality, planning to do with his smuggling friends, when suddenly a voice shouted at me and I turned very fast, to see a gig come racing down the road. It was Ben, his face tight and anxious as he drew up alongside me. I caught my breath — what was he doing here?

'Robyn!' he said, and then gave me a quite unexpected smile. 'Didn't want you to walk home in the dark, so I'm here with the gig. Jump in, maid, and we'll be home before you knows it.' He held out a hand and I just stood there, not knowing what to do.

Clearly, he expected me to be pleased to have a lift back to the inn. But I needed to see Daniel ... Now, as I made no move, his smile died and the old tight look returned. 'Well, get in then ... ' As I still hesitated, he said, looking very suspicious, 'Told Winters, did you, about the lugger? Like I said?'

The rough tone of his voice warned me and suddenly I came to life. I must somehow make him think I had, indeed, told Daniel about the wrong

234

anchorage. I found myself smiling as I climbed into the gig and saying, 'Yes, he'd heard that it was Smuggler's Cove already, so we talked about it.' Which we had done. And now I must pass off this visit to the customs house and keep Ben in a good mood, for I had no idea what he would expect me to do once we were back at the inn.

I told him I'd been to see my ma and my father, and he nodded and said, 'I expect they're pretty proud of you, Robyn, and all you're doing.'

It was hard to answer that, but I mumbled something about them always being glad to see me. He talked as he drove back through the village and up the hill, and I thought he must be in a very good mood. Would I be able to suggest to him that he might stop his smuggling and instead work harder on the cleaning and restoration of the inn? But even as I thought that, I knew it was quite unlikely. Ben was a smuggler through and through, so I would somehow have to follow him into his next free-trading venture in order to help Daniel catch him.

As we drove into the inn yard he said with a chuckle, 'You're a bit quiet, maid. Something upset you, eh?'

I quickly answered, 'I'm tired, Ben. Too much walking this afternoon after all the cleaning. And thank you for coming to fetch me. It was good of you.'

I watched him stable the mare and put the gig into the corner of the yard, and thought how deceitful I was being. For it *was* good of him to drive into the village just to collect me home. Was Ben, after all, a better man that I had thought him? Did he deserve to be arrested and brought up before the magistrate? And then sentenced . . .

Then I had a terrible thought — what if Ben had suspected me of giving him away, and so had come to collect and then imprison me in the Admiral? But, thank goodness, I pushed away the idea and went in to look for Annie.

I was glad to find her in the taproom when I got there. She looked at me and smiled, and I managed during the busy evening to say in her ear, 'I want to talk to you later, before we go to bed. Wait for me in the kitchen.' She nodded, and then I was back behind the counter serving all Ben's mates who had come to make last arrangements for the evening ahead, when the moon would be at its lowest. I felt the warmth of the strip of silk at my breast, and knew I wanted to ask Annie if she recognised any of the pattern of the small piece of lace.

At last it was bedtime, and I persuaded Annie to come upstairs with me where we could talk secretly in my room. I knew she was all agog to know where I had been in the afternoon, so I told her just what Ma and Father had told me, and watched her eyes widen and her mouth drop open. 'Oh, Robyn,' was all she could say as we huddled together on the bed, and I held her hand because she looked so shocked.

Slowly, she came back to life and stared at me. 'You're going to stop smuggling? And try and stop Master as well? How can you do that, Robyn?'

It was a big question, but I had been thinking all the evening between filling the pots and being cheerful to all the men at the bar, and I thought I knew exactly what to do. 'I'm going to Mr Winthrop tomorrow afternoon and tell him and ask for his help. I don't think he's very keen on smuggling himself, and perhaps he'll give me some good advice. And then, of course, I shall go down to the customs house and tell Daniel the truth — that the lugger will anchor in Ness Bay and not at Smugglers' Cove as he had thought.'

'But . . . ' Annie looked worried. 'But what if Master Ben finds out what you're doing? What if he stops you going?'

'Well, then . . . ' I thought about that for a long moment. He couldn't stop me, surely? He had no idea of what I was going to do. I could just leave the inn and do it all; for, after all, I was used to coming and going as I wanted. And Ben had no idea of my plan — did he?

Annie and I looked at each other, and then sat up straight as we heard a footfall outside the door. 'Is that him — listening?' whispered Annie, and we both held our breaths.

After a few moments I realised it was just the old house murmuring as it did of nights. I took out my piece of silk from under my dress and spread it on the bed. 'Look,' I said, 'my mother wrapped me in this before she let me go into the waves. Just look at the lace. Do you recognise any pattern in it? Because if you do, Annie, that might help me find out where I really come from.'

She peered through the candle flame at the lace and then said slowly, 'it looks like something I've seen before, though I can't be sure . . . but I expect Miss Jackson would know. I'll show it to her tomorrow afternoon.'

21

I was up early next morning, planning to slip out and see Mr Winthrop sometime after the midday meal. What I hadn't expected was that Ben would scowl at me as we ate breakfast and say, 'You stay here today, maid. No going off like you do. I need you here.'

I said nothing; just nodded. What was he thinking about? Could he have any idea of my plans? I thought again about him fetching me home last night in the gig, and the expression on his face when he saw me walking through the village: huge frown at first, and then just a bit of a smile. Had he suspected me of anything? Then I remembered that Matt had given him the slip, jumping on a boat off to the Grand Banks — could Ben have thought I might do the same? Not on a boat, of course, but perhaps telling tales to Daniel Winter?

I decided not to say anything, but to appear to agree with what he wanted. I hurried with my breakfast and got Annie washing the dishes quickly, whispering to her that today was going to be difficult; Master Ben was in a bad mood and we must make sure we did nothing to annoy him any further.

As we put all the plates back on the dresser and saw that Mrs Mudge was busy on the fire, slicing up onions for a pie, I said very quietly, 'Come into the scullery. I need to talk to you.'

I saw that Ben was out on the foreshore doing something to his boat, and then he strode back to the stables, so I supposed he would be busy all day preparing for the coming busy night of offloading. When Annie came to my side, eyes wide, I said, 'Don't look so scared! We shall be all right as long as we keep away from Ben. I want you to show Miss Jackson that piece of silk with the lace on it. Ask her if she recognises the pattern, will you? Just think, Annie — a pattern could give me a family name. I mean my real name, not just Lee, like Ma and Father.'

Annie looked shocked. 'But they've been good to you all your life — you wouldn't want to change them, would you?'

That made me think. Of course not; Ma and Father had been real parents to me. But the mystery stayed at the back of my mind all that morning, as I carried on cleaning the upstairs rooms.

At dinner time Ben came into the kitchen and looked at me as I helped Mrs Mudge dish up the meal. 'No going out this afternoon,' he said brusquely as he sat down, and I wondered how I was going to slip away to see Mr Winthrop. It was important to tell him what I badly needed to do — to get a message to Daniel to tell him the real anchorage of the smuggling lugger this evening.

I didn't answer, and at once he swung round, took my shoulder in his big, rough hand and shook me. 'You hear me, Robyn? You stay here where I can see you. Plenty for you to do — getting the cart ready and making sure the other men have got their horses and donkeys ready. We'll be meeting here in the yard, so I can keep my eye on you. Understand?'

In the yard. That meant that the only way of getting the vital news to Daniel was to slip away and go and ask Mr Winthrop to take a message to the customs house. I badly wanted to go myself and tell Daniel, but it didn't seem possible. And yet, all those men coming here with their barrows and carts and horses . . . well, among the noise and the bustle, surely no one would miss me for half an hour, would they? I could run down to the manor house and tell Mr Winthrop. The thought gave me a sudden surge of confidence, and I said very quietly, 'Yes, Ben, I understand. I'll do what you say.'

He grunted, but kept watching me as we finished the meal and cleared up. I told Annie to wait a few minutes until he was busy elsewhere, before leaving for the lace school. 'Come back and go to your room for the evening,' I told her. 'Goodness knows what might be happening here, and I want to make sure you're safe.' She looked a bit frightened but went off happily enough, and then I went out to the yard to busy myself among the men already arriving there with their horses and conveyances.

It was late afternoon when I saw Ben go into the taproom with some of his mates and heard their loud laughter echoing through the yard, and I decided to run. I just prayed that no one saw me — but I was down the lane in no time and then reached Mr Winthrop's big gate safely. I banged on the door and waited impatiently for the maid to let me in.

'I must see Mr Winthrop,' I said in a hurry. 'Tell him it's important.'

She looked a bit cross with me, but disappeared and then came back. 'He's in the garden. He'll see you there. This way.'

At any other time I would have loved to look around in his beautiful garden, so full of trees, bushes and wonderfully colourful flowers. But not today. I went up to him where he was walking away from a gardener, bent double over a flower bed, and said urgently, 'Mr Winthrop, you have to get a message to Daniel Winters at the customs house to tell him that the smugglers are landing at Ness Beach this evening, not in Smuggler's Cove as he thinks. I can't go because Ben Masters won't let me leave the inn — he'll be very angry when he knows I've been here, I'm afraid. But I had to come.'

He looked at me with his black eyes and I saw a new expression on his long, lean face. He seemed more friendly, I thought. 'Then it's brave of you to come, Robyn,' he said soberly. 'Yes, I'll drive straight down to the village and give Winters your message. You're quite sure of what you're doing, are you?

Because of course this means Martin and his band will be involved in a fight, and possibly gaoled. Is this what you really want?'

I met his keen gaze and allowed myself to think once again — did I want Ben to go to gaol? Well, all that I knew was that I needed the smuggling to stop. There must be no more wrecked ships; no more orphan babies rescued from towering waves by one kindly village man. I found I was suddenly weeping. Tears seared my cheeks and I felt sobs wracking my chest.

Mr Winthrop put his arms around me. 'My dear child! Come and sit down.' He led me to a wooden bench and there I collapsed, telling him about my rescue by Father, and my real mother's awful death by drowning. 'Wreckers!' I sobbed. 'And smugglers stealing the drowning people's rings and jewelry. It mustn't go on, Mr Winthrop. Please help me try and stop it!'

He sat beside me, gave me his white

handkerchief to dry my cheeks, and then slowly said, 'Strange you should decide to do this, Robyn. For I have come to the same conclusion over the last few days. Smuggling has had its day, I believe, for taxes are being lowered and the demand will no longer be there. And I'm very interested in the fact that you are a child of someone drowned on our beach. Perhaps we can try and find out the name of the ship, which will give us a list of passengers. Now dry your tears, and yes, of course I'll drive down and tell Daniel Winters. But I'm worried about you going back to the inn. Do you think Martin will have missed you being away for this short time? And if I drive you there, can you slip in without being seen?'

I was instantly cheered by all he had said and so was able to get up and smile at him. 'Thank you, Mr Winthrop. Yes, I expect I can just run into the inn without any of those noisy men seeing me. They'll be busy drinking now.'

He left me at a place behind the

hedge near the entrance to the inn, telling me to stay indoors during the evening and not think of going down to Ness Beach. 'Tell Martin you feel unwell. He can't make you go, and anyway that will be no place for a girl at such a time.'

I wondered how I was going to explain to Ben that I wasn't going to help while they unloaded the contraband from the ship. I wasn't sure, but I knew Mr Winthrop must hurry up and get down to Daniel, so I just said, 'I'll try and do as you say, and thank you for helping me, sir.'

He gave me a long look and his smile grew warm. As he lifted the whip to get the pony going again, he said quietly, 'I don't think you should call me 'sir', Robyn, but that's something we must try and discover later on. I'll get down to the customs house now.'

I watched him drive away down the lane towards the village, and felt thankful to know that Daniel would get the message in good time to muster his troops and be ready for Ben and his band of rough men when they reached Ness Beach later on this evening. But now I had the job of trying to get into the inn without anyone seeing me . . .

I was just entering the inn when a roar of a voice stopped me. 'Robyn! Where've you been? Come here, gel. I'll teach you to slope off like that . . . ' A heavy arm wrapped itself around my waist and suddenly I was almost lifted off my feet, propelled down the passage and up the dark staircase. 'I'll put you where you won't go off again. I got a nice little hidey-hole in the attic, where you'll just stay put and I'll know where you be . . . '

He was taking me to the hole Annie had discovered. I was going to be his prisoner, and there seemed nothing I could do to stop him.

22

I was so shocked my wits deserted me — but only for a few seconds. He began pushing me up the stairs, and I suddenly remembered how I fell here, into Daniel's arms. That was just what I needed to turn round, thinking wildly, *Daniel. I must get away from Ben and find you* . . . I gave Ben an almighty shove and, taken by surprise, he fell backwards, shouting as he did so. But I didn't listen. Somehow I managed to get past him, down the passage, out of the door and into the yard, running as I had never run in my life before. For, even if Ben was hurt and so unable to chase me, then surely some of his drinking mates in the taproom, would come to his help and do so.

I ran and ran, never looking back, getting more and more out of breath, but telling myself, *Go on, go on*. Only when I was unable to take another breath without coughing and coming to a helpless standstill, did I stop. Here in the lane going down towards the village, all was quiet. A lark spiraled over the field. I heard a dog bark in someone's farm, and then I was able to tell myself I had escaped; Ben wasn't coming after me. Relief swept through me and I decided I would just have a little rest, and then go on down to find Daniel.

I found myself near the Holy Well so, remembering its atmosphere of peace, I went to the wellhead and sank down on the rich green turf. Quietness. Security. I was safe. No one chasing me. But then there was the sound of horse's hooves approaching, and I jumped. Some one coming nearer and nearer . . .

The hedge moved. A rider and his horse came around it, and I was looking into the keen sea-green eyes of Daniel Winters. 'Oh!' I said, and then stood silent, hardly believing that he was here.

He tethered the horse and came to my side. We looked at each other and I saw a new expression on his face, one that I hadn't seen before: warmth and concern. I took a big breath and said unevenly, 'I was coming to find you, Daniel,' and then stopped as he took my hands in his and drew me towards him.

There was worry in his quick words. 'Are you safe? Ben Martin hasn't hurt you, Robyn? Winthrop has told me about the anchorage at Ness Beach tonight, and I had to come at once and see that you were safe. He was afraid Martin might discover that you had informed me about the smuggling and done something to hurt you.'

I smiled as all my fears vanished. 'I'm quite all right,' I said quietly, and he nodded then.

'Thank goodness. And what have you to tell me about yourself? You won't be at the beach tonight, I hope and pray? I have mustered a large troop of men, all armed, and there's bound to be a fight while we round up all the smugglers.' His voice dropped and he added gently, 'I don't want you there, dear maid.'

He was looking at me with such care in his eyes that I could find no words to tell him just what I was feeling. That Daniel should call me 'dear maid' suddenly gave me another view of life. *He cared*, and that meant all the world to me. My dream was coming true!

I could only shake my head and smile at him, wishing the words would come. And then, suddenly, they did. 'Daniel' I said unsteadily, 'I shall be at the beach tonight, but not because I'm with the smugglers. I shall come to make sure that you are safe. You see, I've learned that my mother was drowned by smugglers who wrecked the ship she was traveling in, and I was picked out of the waves by the man who became my dear father, Robert Lee. So I'll never have sympathy with smugglers again.'

He took a huge breath and I saw wonder fill his eyes — wonder and a new shining light that told me of his pleasure. He drew me very close so that I felt his heart beating beneath his blue coat, and whispered into my hair, 'You poor child, discovering that. But the way you feel about smuggling now is what I've been praying for — praying and hoping, Robyn. You see, although we haven't been together very often, I have grown so fond of you. I think of you when I should be doing other things.' His voice was muffled. 'I long to see you and to hold you, like this.'

We were together, in each other's arms, and I knew that I was safe and loved. And that I need have no fears about the future. But then thoughts of Annie came into my mind and I stepped away from him. 'I feel that, too, Daniel. I think of you so much, so often. But now I still have something I must do. So I must go.'

He was frowning. I watched his arms drop to his side and felt a pang of loneliness. 'What must you do?' he asked sharply.

It was so hard to tell him. All I

wanted was to stay there — close to him, part of him, part of my dream come true, knowing my worries were over. But they weren't; not quite. Thoughts of Annie, of the Admiral, of Mrs Mudge suddenly overcame my selfish longings, and I was able to say quietly, 'I must go and meet Annie from her lace school and take her to my mother's cottage. Ma and Father have promised to take her in, you see. And then — ' It was hard to say this bit. I breathed in heavily and then said, 'I shall go back to the inn and let Ben think I'm still on his side. I don't want him to change his plans, not now that you know where the real anchorage is to be.' I looked into his suddenly narrowed eyes and realised that this was very difficult for both of us. Would he believe me? Would he try and stop me?

It was a few seconds before he spoke, and then he slowly nodded, saying, 'I don't want you to do this, Robyn. I shall worry while you're gone.' His voice deepened and he frowned. 'And if that rogue Ben Martin raises a finger against you, I'll make sure he gets his just deserts. But, dear maid, I trust you.' He was smiling again and my heart stopped racing. 'And I know you are loyal to what you see as your duties,' he went on. 'So very well. But let me take you down to the village to find Annie. Come, you shall ride the mare and I'll lead you. Let me help you up.'

I was up on the mare's back, helped by those two warm, strong arms. With Daniel walking beside me, we started down the lane to the village. I would be in time, I knew, to find Annie and to take her to Apple Cottage. But then I would have to leave all my loved ones and walk alone back to the inn, where I would find Ben and his rough mates waiting. And how would he greet me? I wondered nervously.

23

Ben greeted me with a scowl and I knew from his breath that he'd been drinking. 'Back again, eh?' he shouted unsteadily, but then he walked away, saying over his shoulder, 'Well, at least you're here in time to help with the horses. Get yourself ready; it'll be dark soon and we'll be moving.'

I went up to my room and found my old coat and battered hat. It would be windy on the beach, and also I didn't want anyone to recognise me. I pinned up my hair really tightly and then made my way down to the taproom, where I was able to have a few moments' peace while the men went outside and got ready to make the journey down to the village and the beach. Mrs Mudge had already gone home, and I had met Annie and taken her to Apple Cottage where Ma and Father welcomed her, and I knew she would be looked after and loved from now on. And Daniel cared for me. My mind cleared, and I was smiling as I joined the men in the yard. It was just me and the offloading to think about now — and being with Daniel amidst all the danger.

Not much later, a small procession headed out of the yard, down the track and into the lane leading to the village: horses and carts, a couple of gigs pulled by donkeys, and at least three or four men with ponies. All the men carried either staves or clubs, and even a musket or two. I didn't look at them, for they were signs of what I feared would be violence. Ben told me to sit with him as he drove Lady, who pulled the cart. I guessed that he was glad to have someone sitting beside him in Matt's place, but I said nothing as we jolted along and I kept thinking about Daniel waiting down by the beach with his troop of men. Armed men, he had said, which was a horrible thought. But I knew it had to be faced, and I prayed that no one would be hurt.

Darkness had really fallen by the time we drove through the village and on towards the tunnel cut out of the cliff, through which we entered Ness Beach. Wheels rattled in the blackness of the tunnel, adding to the frightening feeling that was slowly creeping through me, and by the time we came out of the dark onto the shadowy beach I had to blink a few times to adjust my sight. There was no moonlight, but a couple of swaying lanterns which showed me glimpses of a huge ship anchored just offshore. Its sails were flapping as it headed into the rising wind, and I knew it was the lugger with the contraband.

Now the carts were standing on the beach. Ben told me to stay with Lady, and also hold the reins of several of the other horses and ponies whose riders were making ready to unload the small dinghy I saw making its way through the waves towards the beach. There was a wind gusting now, and I saw how the swell mounted, making it hard for the rowers of the boat to reach the shore. But there were strong arms pulling it in, and very soon the unloading started.

I stood by the horses given to my care, holding their reins and making sure their big hooves didn't tread on me as they moved restlessly around. I watched as barrels were rolled ashore and stowed in carts. Packages and small tubs were loaded onto the broad backs of donkeys in the crooks hung from their saddles and in the gigs, and soon the beach was busy with men taking delivery of a huge load of contraband. What was it all? I wondered. Rum, of course, and brandy in the barrels; silks, laces, even rare stones and snuff packed in the parcels and packages; and tobacco in huge casks. What a prize for Ben and his mates, if they got away with it. But that made my thoughts turn back to Daniel and his men. Where were they? Had he decided not to come?

Even as I wondered, I heard the clatter of many hooves down the tunnel, and then saw several lanterns lighting up the scene on the beach. I held my breath as Daniel rode up to Ben, who was lifting a big tub into the cart, and shouted loudly, 'In the name of the king, I arrest you and your men, Ben Martin. Give up your arms and surrender your illegal goods, or it'll be the worse for you.'

Ben shoved the tub into the cart, turned and scowled at Daniel. 'You'll have to fight us if you want us to give up these goods. Keep out of the way, or we'll get our muskets out.' He gestured with his left arm and at once there was the sound of men shouting abuse, followed by a flurry of stones aimed at the troop of customs men.

I felt my body tense and wished that I was a man, so that I could deliver a good strong blow to Ben and make him realise he was outnumbered. But Daniel's response was simply to repeat his words and pull at the reins of his horse, which reared up, making Ben step backwards. He shouted to his men to attack, and then there were fights breaking out all over the beach.

I pulled the horses out of the way and retreated to the shelter of the cliffs, wishing I had never got involved in this awful free-trading. I realised now that I had been foolish, not thinking what the outcome of my actions might be. Now Ben and his men were facing up to Daniel, still mounted, with his little troop of men all around him. Clubs were raised and blows struck, and I hardly dared look in case of accidents; but through the darkness I could only see clubs and staves waving about the men's heads, and Daniel's mounted men leaning down and making attempts to arrest the smugglers.

Then Daniel saw me. He spurred on his horse, came to where I cowered in the shadows and bent down. 'Why are you here? You shouldn't have come. Leave those horses and go back through the tunnel. This is no place for a woman.'

His tone made me feel useless, and I

heard my voice rise as I answered back: 'I can't leave them. They'll run off and get lost, or hurt.'

His answer was lost as a musket was fired. I saw him turn in the saddle, then race back to the fray of struggling men and horses. That was enough for me. I decided what I must do, which was to save the horses. So I tried my hardest to persuade them to follow me through the tunnel, and finally out onto the road leading to the beach. There we stopped, my heart racing as I heard more musket fire and began imagining terrible injuries to anyone in that muddle of fighting men. What if Daniel was hurt? Suppose Ben was killed? Why, oh why had I got into this awful situation in the first place?

And then, into my chaotic mind came the sound of running footsteps down the tunnel. I peered through the darkness and saw a figure — a man clutching a club and carrying a pistol, and recognised Ben. He came up to where I waited, half-hidden in the shadows, stared wildly, and then said, 'Got the horses, have you? Bring Lady here; hold my club while I get on.'

For a moment I simply stood there not knowing what to do. Was he running away? And should I help him? Then I thought of Daniel and all the other men — preventive men and smuggling friends of Ben — still fighting on the beach, and knew I must do something to force Ben to stay and help his mates. I said angrily, 'You can't just go like this! What about your friends? And all the cargo that's being landed from the lugger? If you disappear, Daniel will arrest them and they'll be blamed for all the work that you planned. Don't be such a coward, Ben Martin!'

His scowl grew huge, and he raised an arm and hit out at me. I ducked, but too late; his knobbly fist landed on my head and pain swept through me like a surging wave. I felt my legs waver beneath me, and before I knew anything else I was falling, and then it all went black.

How long it was that I lay there on the road in the darkness, I had no idea. All I knew was that magical moment of semi-consciousness when I felt someone lift me and I was carried for a few minutes; I felt the warmth of a human body. Then I heard a man's voice that I recognised — was it Mr Winthrop? — saying, 'Put the blanket around her, Winters. That's it, make her comfortable on the long seat. I'll drive her home to her parents' cottage in the village. And what about you? Get that nasty wound looked at, and let your men deal with the prisoners.'

My aching head didn't know what to make of all that, but one word became important as I grew more aware of what was happening. *A nasty wound* . . . Daniel, wounded? At once I struggled to sit up, but now I realised I was in Mr Winthrop's gig and he was driving carefully along the road through the darkness, heading for Apple Cottage.

Somehow I managed to sit up properly and, pushing aside the blanket wrapped around me, leaned forward to touch Mr Winthrop's arm. 'Please,' I said faintly. 'Please tell me that Daniel is all right. And that Ben didn't get away.' But my voice faded and I had to lie down again or collapse.

Through a sort of dreaminess I heard Mr Winthrop say, 'Don't worry about anything, Robyn. I'm taking you home where your mother will look after you. That must've been a very hard bang on the head, and you need to rest. We'll talk about Winters and Martin later when you feel better. Now just lie back and stop worrying.'

I did lie back, because I had no strength to do anything else; but the jolting of the gig kept me awake, and all I could think of was his last words: 'Stop worrying.' This seemed ridiculous, because of course I was worried. Ben Martin, bad as he was, probably arrested and facing a big sentence . . . and my beloved Daniel wounded. *A nasty wound*, Mr Winthrop had said. Of course all I could do was lie there and worry.

24

Such a fuss was being made of me! Next morning Ma and Father stood beside the bed with worried eyes, until I managed a smile and said weakly, 'I'm all right now. It was only a bit of a bang. And Mr Winthrop has been wonderful — is he here?'

Father knelt down at my side and reached to hold my hands. 'The gentleman has gone to see how the customs officer is. Apparently he was wounded. I expect he'll come back later.'

Annie, at the foot of the bed, smiled as she whispered, 'And I've got some news about that piece of lace, Robyn. But it'll wait till you feel better.'

I knew I must stay here, for my mind was still echoing with gunfire and shouting voices, and I found it hard to think of anything else. But slowly that faded, and then the one thought that came, dark and worrying, was that of Daniel being wounded.

Ma and Father had gone downstairs, and Annie had tidied my bed and plumped up my pillow, smiling as she said, 'I help Ma with the vegetables — better than those old pots! And she says it'll be my birthday tomorrow . . . ' She skipped from the room, and I knew it was time to get up and face whatever might come next. I wanted to be dressed and ready for anything when Mr Winthrop came to tell me the news about Daniel.

My head ached a bit, but once I was up I felt stronger. Downstairs I told Ma not to worry, and went into the garden where I sat on the bench under the apple tree. When I heard the gig halt outside the gate I got up and went quickly down the path.

Mr Winthrop dismounted and came towards me. He smiled. 'Feeling better?' he asked, and I nodded and smiled.

'Yes, thank you. And thank you for

saving me last night. But please — have you any news of Daniel?' My voice wobbled. 'Is he badly hurt?'

Mr Winthrop's smile was almost a grin. 'Wait and see. He insisted on walking here. Wouldn't have a lift with me — said it would get his strength back to use his legs.'

My heart leaped and I had to take an extra big breath before saying, 'So his wound wasn't too bad? And he can walk? And he's *coming here?*'

'Of course. He's worried about you. Said you should never have been on the beach last night. Which I agree with. Why did you go, Robyn?'

I hung my head. 'I know it was foolish. But I had to be there, knowing that Daniel would be in danger . . . '

Mr Winthrop said gently, 'So that's how things are between you. Well, I wish you both well. And now I must return to the customs house, as I have something I need to do there. Good day, Robyn, and I shall look forward to seeing you again soon.'

'Thank you, Mr Winthrop. Yes, I hope to be back at the Admiral before too long. There's so much still to do there, and perhaps Ben will be there, too . . . '

He cleared his throat and said quickly, 'I shouldn't rely on that. But Winters will tell you what is happening.' He gave me a last smile and returned to his gig outside the gate.

I stayed under the apple tree and tried to sort out my raging thoughts. Had Ben been arrested? And when would Daniel come? Did he need to see me so badly that he was ignoring his wound? Restlessly, after a few moments, I returned to the cottage to find Annie beating up eggs and Ma creaming butter and sugar.

'My birthday cake!' trilled Annie with a huge smile. 'Ma says it'll be a party at the end of this week.'

'That's lovely,' I said, glad that a happy moment was coming in spite of all these worries surrounding me. I remembered then what Annie had said about the lace on my piece of old silk and said curiously, 'You were going to tell me something about the lace. What was it?'

She put down her spoon and looked across the table at me. 'Miss Jackson recognised the pattern, Robyn. She said it was one belonging to a local family called Martin.'

'Martin!' I was speechless for a moment. 'But Annie, that's Ben's name!'

'Is it?' she said, going back to beating the eggs. 'Oh yes, Master Ben Martin — I remember now.' She stopped again. 'Miss Jackson said it must belong to someone in Captain Martin's family. Who do you think it could have been, Robyn?'

'I don't know.' But something was running around my brain: the portrait of a young woman in the captain's room at the inn. The lady with the handsome lace collar to her dress, and the pale hair that Mr Winthrop had suggested was like mine. What else had he said? . . . That there was a resemblance. Did that mean I was like the lady in the portrait? But how could I be?

I had to sit down quickly. Ma stopped her beating and came over to me. 'You look pale, love. Sit down quietly and let's forget all this rubbish about lace.'

'But Ma, I don't think it is rubbish.' Somehow small bits of something were starting to fit together. 'I think there may be something important in it . . . '

There was a knock at the door and a deep voice said, 'May I come in?'

'Oh,' I gasped, jumping up, going to the door and opening it. 'Yes, please come in, Mr Winters . . . ' I met his eyes, sea-green and very wide, looking at me in a way that sent the blood surging through my whole body.

'Robyn, thank heavens you're safe and well.' He held out a hand, which I took as I smiled.

'Quite well, Daniel. But what about you? Your wound — ?'

His answering smile banished all my

worries. 'Just a flesh wound. The musket ball only grazed my arm. But you look pale, Robyn. Surely you should sit down.'

Ma was standing beside me, eyes wide as she took in Daniel's expression. 'So this is the customs officer — Mr Winters, is it?'

'Yes, Ma. Mr Winters was wounded in the battle on Ness Beach last night.'

She didn't let me finish. 'When you were hit by that ruffian, Ben Martin. What a to-do!'

Daniel nodded and said gently, 'But it's all over now, Mrs Lee. And how thankful I am to find Robyn is getting over the wretch's blow. He's in the lock-up with several of his mates, and will be taken up to Exeter prison shortly for trial before the magistrate.'

I caught my breath. 'Poor Ben,' I breathed, and Daniel frowned.

'Not so poor. He would have got away with a massive load of contraband if you hadn't helped me get the venue right, Robyn. But there's something I must tell you.' He glanced around the cottage, then said with a warm smile, 'As your mother and Annie seem to be very busy, shall we go outside and talk without bothering them?'

'Of course, Daniel. Ma, we shall only be in the garden.'

We walked slowly up the brick path to the bench under the apple tree, and he sat me down carefully as if I were a piece of china, I thought. Already my headache was going, and I had a new wonderful hope that things might be going in a way which my dreams had longed for. Daniel and I, talking together; his hand holding mine, his eyes not leaving my own.

When we were settled, he said, 'I have a message to give you from Ben Martin.' His smile flowered. 'Don't look surprised. He's a scheming chap, and has already got ideas about getting free of a possible sentence by the court. You see, he feels very bad about hitting you as he did, and wants you to know how sorry he is. He said something about you being his girl . . . '

Now Daniel's smile died and he frowned, so I said quickly, 'No, no, I wasn't.'

'I'm glad to hear it, because I like to think you're my girl. Are you, Robyn?' The smile returned and he pressed my hand.

My dream was coming true. I felt happiness soar through me and all I could whisper was, 'Yes, Daniel. Oh, yes!'

The rest of the day disappeared in a shaft of sunlight. Daniel had to return to the customs house, but said he would come back very soon as he needed to talk to Father. In the late afternoon Mr Winthrop appeared, his face full of something which excited me.

'Are you well enough to come with me, Robyn? We need to go the Admiral, for I think I have news for you.' He looked over my shoulder to where Annie was standing by the fire. 'And you must come, too, Annie. It's all to do with lace, you see.'

I hardly knew what I was doing, with Daniel saying he needed to talk to Father, and I couldn't let myself hope that I guessed why; and now Mr Winthrop had some news, too. We sat in the gig, waiting impatiently for the inn to come into view, and then climbed out, Mr Winthrop taking us into the captain's room.

He sat us down around the table and then said, 'I believe you have a scrap of lace, Robyn, which was on your body when you were saved from the waves. Have you got it with you?'

I took it out of my dress and smoothed it down, looking at the lace edging with excitement. What might this be about to tell me?

Mr Winthrop stood beneath the portrait of the woman with the lace collar and said very solemnly, 'Robyn, with Daniel's help I have been searching the lists of locally wrecked ships and have found that a member of the Martin family — a young woman, with a child — was sailing in the *Medusa*, wrecked on the black rocks in that bad storm seventeen years ago. And now, with Annie telling us about the lace pattern belonging to the Martin family, I think we can complete the whole story.' He moved towards me and put his hands on my shoulders, saying gently, 'Robyn, my dear, when I said there was a likeness to this woman in the portrait, I was right. I know now that she was Elsa Prince, a younger married sister of Captain Martin's, sailing here on holiday, bringing you to meet your uncle. So you see, you are his niece. Not Robyn Lee, but Robyn Prince.'

His voice died away and I was left surrounded by silence and clamouring thoughts. My mother, drowned; dear Father saving me and bringing me up in the Lee family. How blessed I had been, but how wonderful to know the truth. Of course it made no difference to my feelings for Ma and Father, but it made a difference to me, for I now knew that I was someone in my own right.

I was silent, trying to keep back the threatening tears, and glad of Mr Winthrop's warm hand on my shoulder. Annie slid her hand into mine, and whispered, 'Sounds like your dream is coming true, Robyn. And what about Mr Winters?'

That broke the spell and at once I got up and said, 'I can't thank you enough, Mr Winthrop. And now I must go back and tell Ma and Father . . . '

'Of course,' he said with a smile. 'I'll take you both home.'

At Apple Cottage another surprise awaited me. Daniel was in the garden, talking to Father, and smiled as he turned. He came to the gate and put his arms around me. 'Robyn, I have something amazing to tell you. Ben Martin has written you a note. Here it is.'

It was a crumpled bit of paper with bad writing scribbled across it, the words hard to read. But I managed. Ben said:

Robyn, maid, I'm going to join Matt in the cod fishing, so you can have the Admiral. You'll run it well. It's the reward I said you must have. Ben Martin.

I stared at Daniel. 'But he's in prison — how can he possibly go to the Grand Banks?'

Daniel smiled and said, 'I told you he had a scheme to work out. Well, this is it: some of his friends broke in and rescued him — slippery as an eel, that man. Another escape in the customs records, I'm afraid.'

I stood there gaping, and then he put his arms around me and said very quietly, 'Now, Robyn, shall we ride up to the Admiral? For I have something important to ask you. Will you come with me?'

I had no answer, so just nodded and closed my eyes. Ma and Father watched us ride away. They waved and I leaned back against Daniel's strong, warm body, hoping that the question he had asked Father was the one he would soon ask me.

It was. Reaching the Admiral — my inn from now on, I thought with growing pride and excitement — we then dismounted on the foreshore. We sat on the coarse, warm sand, watching the river flow past us — quiet, strong and beautiful — and Daniel spoke in his deep, low voice the words I had been longing to hear: 'Robyn, will you do me the honour of marrying me? May I be your helpful landlord as you take over this old inn and turn it into the place you have been planning ever since you came here?'

There was only one answer, and I made it instantly. 'Yes, Daniel! Oh yes, that will be wonderful!'

He pulled me closer and kissed me, and I knew then that in this magical moment all my dreams had finally come true.

We do hope that you have enjoyed reading this large print book.

Did you know that all of our titles are available for purchase?

We publish a wide range of high quality large print books including:
Romances, Mysteries, Classics
General Fiction
Non Fiction and Westerns

Special interest titles available in large print are:
The Little Oxford Dictionary
Music Book, Song Book
Hymn Book, Service Book

Also available from us courtesy of Oxford University Press:
Young Readers' Dictionary
(large print edition)
Young Readers' Thesaurus
(large print edition)

For further information or a free brochure, please contact us at:
Ulverscroft Large Print Books Ltd.,
The Green, Bradgate Road, Anstey,
Leicester, LE7 7FU, England.
Tel: (00 44) **0116 236 4325**
Fax: (00 44) **0116 234 0205**

VALENTINE MASQUERADE

Margaret Sutherland

New Year's Eve is hot and sultry in more ways than one when a tall, handsome prince fixes the newest lady in his court with a magnetic gaze. Who could say no to a prince — especially a charmer like Will Bradshaw? Caitlin has to wonder. And Will wonders, too, if he might have finally found the woman to banish the hurts of years gone by. But what if the one ill-judged mistake of Caitlin's past happens to be the single fault he can't accept?